As far as she was concerned, Sawyer Huffman already had three strikes against him.

The bad history between their families, their professional conflicts and a child.

And that counted him out as a relationship prospect regardless of his appeal.

It was just that he did have appeal.

So, so much appeal…

But she wasn't going to let that get to her. No way, no how.

Because as determined as she was to get this job she'd been given done, she was even more determined about that!

* * *

The Camdens of Colorado:
They've made a fortune in business.
Can they make it in the game of love?

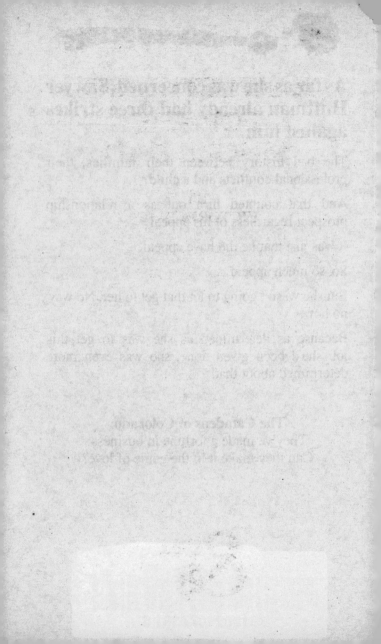

A SWEETHEART FOR THE SINGLE DAD

BY
VICTORIA PADE

MILLS & BOON

Published in Great Britain 2015
by Mills & Boon, an imprint of Harlequin (UK) Limited,
Eton House, 18-24 Paradise Road, Richmond, Surrey, TW9 1SR

© 2015 Victoria Pade

ISBN: 978-0-263-25168-5

23-0915

Harlequin (UK) Limited's policy is to use papers that are natural, renewable and recyclable products and made from wood grown in sustainable forests. The logging and manufacturing processes conform to the legal environmental regulations of the country of origin.

Printed and bound in Spain
by CPI, Barcelona

Victoria Pade is a *USA TODAY* bestselling author. A native of Colorado, she's lived there her entire life. She studied art before discovering her real passion was for writing, and even after more than eighty books, she still loves it. When she isn't writing she's baking and worrying about how to work off the calories. She has better luck with the baking than with the calories. Readers can contact her on her Facebook page.

Chapter One

"You're a Camden. Shall I guess which one?"

It was late on Monday afternoon, the last day of August, when Lindie Camden went into the recreation room of the Wheatley Community Center and someone stepped up behind her to speak those words.

The voice was male, deep and rich. The tone was slightly confrontational, slightly facetious, and so low that no one else was likely to hear despite the fact that there were a number of other adults and children all around.

Lindie wasn't sure whether it was good or bad that she'd been sort of recognized. She was on a mission today from her grandmother to connect with Sawyer Huffman and attempt to take the thorn out of the lion's paw once and for all.

She'd tried calling to request an appointment to see

him. But she'd been informed that Sawyer Huffman was not interested in hearing anything a Camden might have to say.

Undeterred, at lunch she'd gone home to change into her tightest pencil skirt, a sleeveless silk top with a cowl neck that flowed with some intriguing folds in front, and a pair of four-inch, come-and-get-it spiked heels.

She'd left her long, espresso-brown hair to fall loosely to the middle of her back the way she would wear it to go clubbing. She'd applied shadow, liner and mascara to her cerulean-blue eyes. She'd dusted her cheeks and her thin nose with a hint more color. Then she'd added her favorite rose-hued lipstick to lips that were naturally full. All to present herself at the offices of Huffman Consulting and hopefully lure him into meeting with her, appointment or not.

That scheme had at least gained her information from a young male intern that Sawyer Huffman had left for the day to volunteer at the community center in Wheatley, a suburb about twenty minutes outside Denver.

The intractably determined Lindie had come straight here and told the person at the front desk only that she was looking for Sawyer Huffman. She'd been informed that he could be found in the recreation room at the chess tables.

It was the chess tables she was looking for when the near-whisper had come from behind.

Lindie turned to face tall, not-too-dark but very, very handsome Sawyer Huffman himself.

The arch nemesis of Camden Superstores.

And the son of a man who had been a victim of some underhanded actions on the part of the previous generation's Camdens.

As one of Camden Incorporated's most outspoken opponents, Lindie had seen Sawyer Huffman's picture in newspapers and magazines; she'd seen him interviewed and in news reports on television. It had been obvious that he was attractive.

But he was a lot more impressive in person.

Standing six-foot-three, he was a big guy all the way around. There didn't seem to be an ounce of fat behind the suit pants and dress shirt he was wearing. He had a broad chest and shoulders, thick forearms showing from beneath sleeves rolled to his elbows, and massive hands that grasped muscular arms he crossed over his flat middle.

He was kind of daunting even though she didn't see any anger or resentment on his gorgeous face. He had light brown hair that he wore short on the sides and only a bit longer and carelessly kept on top. His finely angular features included just-high-enough cheekbones, a sharp jawline and a nose with just enough of a ridge in the bridge to give him a roguish air.

His lower lip was fuller than his upper and there were the sexiest little parentheses at their corners, drawn there at that moment by his questioning Cheshire-cat smile. He also had a slightly crooked crease in the center of his square-ish chin and amazing crystal-blue eyes. Eyes filled with curiosity now as he gazed down at her, waiting for her response.

"I'm Lindie," she said simply.

"I figured. A phone call this morning asking to meet with me and now you've tracked me down here? Are you the family assassin?" he asked, the thought seeming to amuse him.

"Not today. I left all my weapons at home" was Lindie's comeback.

Her clothing choice wasn't lost on him because his glance dropped for a split second before he said, "I'm not so sure about that."

Then the tone that had held a mingling of admiration and suspicion became more businesslike. "I came here to run a chess tournament for these kids, so I don't know what you're up to but—"

"I'm not *up to* anything. I'm representing my family's company. We'd like to improve relations with you and to hire you. But since you wouldn't see me at your office—"

"*Improve relations* with me? *Hire* me?" he repeated as if she were out of her mind. "Neither of those things is ever going happen, *Ms.* Camden. It's my *job* to be your adversary. A job I created and have no intention of changing."

"Lindie. I'm just Lindie," she corrected.

"It's my job to be your adversary, *Lindie,*" he reiterated as if she might understand it better that way.

Huffman Consulting represented several of Camden Superstores' competitors—major grocery store, home improvement and department store chains. Every time an area was targeted as the site for a new Camden Superstore, Huffman Consulting went to work to present the downside on behalf of their clients in an effort to raise community support to keep out the superstore.

Through pamphlets, phone calls, news reports, petition drives, websites and contact with big and small local businesses and homeowners, Huffman Consulting spread the word that the arrival of a Camden Superstore lowered property values, drove out small businesses, increased traffic congestion and police calls, and caused any number of other evils.

The campaigns often either kept the Camdens from opening a store at all, or caused lengthy, expensive delays while the company's PR team worked to combat the campaign and win over the communities.

"If Camden Incorporated became one of your clients it would be your job to represent *our* interests, as well," Lindie said reasonably.

"You want me in bed with the enemy," he countered.

Ooh. That put a saucy image in her head that came out of nowhere and shouldn't have been there!

Lindie shoved it away and reminded herself that this was solely about business.

"What we want is not to *be* your enemy," she said. "It's only recently come to our attention that some…questionable *things* were done years ago to your family. We understand that that's probably left you thinking badly of us and wanting to get even. But we'd like to clear the air and compensate you by way of our business—always worth a substantial amount of money."

"What is this? The Camdens' own twelve-step program? Are you on the admit-wrongdoing-and-make-amends part?"

In truth the Camdens *were* trying to make amends to people who had been wronged by Lindie's predecessors. But they also didn't want that widely known and inspiring false allegations.

So Lindie ignored the questions and said, "Give me a chance. Get to know me and Camden Incorporated *through* me. Let me get to know you and where you're really coming from. Then maybe we can find common ground and work together."

"*This* is where I'm really coming from," he said with a gesture around the community center. "Areas like this eastern side of Wheatley that are left behind when a Camden Superstore comes to town. When jobs are lost and businesses close and buildings go vacant. When resources are drained away to the more prosperous parts of town. When parents have to take jobs farther away from home so their commute is longer and more time is taken away from their kids. Kids who are ultimately left with less supervision, leading them to get into trouble. Kids who need somewhere to go that isn't an empty house or apartment."

Okay, the man didn't pull any punches. But Lindie could take them.

Before she'd thought of something diplomatic to say he added, "You want to get to know what I'm after? Pitch in here. Volunteer. Learn firsthand what the Camdens leave in their dust. Make some *real* amends to people you've done harm to right now."

It was a dare. A dare he clearly thought Lindie wouldn't accept.

He couldn't have been more wrong. Jumping in to help was her middle name. Sometimes to her own detriment.

But her goal today was strictly to connect with him. To get some time with him. That was the only hope she had of turning him from an enemy to an ally.

So rather than immediately accepting his challenge, she wanted to make sure it would get her what she needed.

"Do you 'pitch in' here? Volunteer—beyond your chess tournament today?" she asked.

"I have connections to Wheatley and this community center happens to be my pet project, so, yes, I volunteer here."

"What kind of connections? Do you live in Wheatley?"

"I live in a loft in lower downtown Denver. But my son lives here."

"You have a son?" she said, hoping to build some rapport even as she took particular note of that fact for her own personal reasons. The fact that he had a child helped put him all the more securely in the wouldn't-date-him compartment and she thought that that should help her concentrate on the work at hand.

"I do have a son," he answered. "Sam. He lives in Wheatley with his mother and her new husband. For now."

He seemed compelled to add that last part, though it was under his breath. Unsure how to reply, she merely said, "You're divorced?"

"As a matter of fact I am. But not from Sam's mom. She and I were never married."

Divorced, with a child with a woman from a different relationship. The man seemed to have quite a history.

"Does your son use the community center?" she asked.

"He's four and in the preschool program here. But the center is also important because if the older kids have a place they want to spend time, it keeps them off the streets and out of trouble. Ultimately that makes things safer and better for Sam. Plus, there's the park the center just acquired next door—he'll like that when it's in shape."

"So other than the chess tournament, what do you do as a volunteer here?" she persisted.

"I come in every Thursday afternoon—today is a special occasion for the tournament—and spend time with the kids themselves. Other than that I do whatever I can.

Right now we need community involvement in cleaning up the park. So tomorrow I'm going door-to-door with flyers to get the word out. The most immediate project is rehabbing the park itself—work on that starts Friday afternoon at one. Schools around here are having an early release that day, so we're doing a lunch for the kids, then putting everybody at the center to work and hoping for outside help, too."

"So this week you'll be here tomorrow handing out flyers, then again on Thursday and Friday?" Lindie summarized for clarity.

"Are you setting up a timetable to stalk me? Because if you're around here, I'll get you involved," he warned.

"Let's say I'm fine with that. What would you get me involved doing? Could I hand out flyers with you? Do whatever you do with the kids on Thursdays? Work by your side on the park cleanup?"

"You want to be my shadow?" he said as if that amused him once more.

"I was just thinking that I could kill two birds with one stone. If volunteering gives me the chance to talk to you, I'm happy to volunteer."

"Talking to me isn't going to do you any good." Another warning.

"I can be very persuasive."

"Ah. The Camden persuader not the Camden assassin. I can relax."

"Because I obviously had you terrified."

He laughed. "You can tag along tomorrow. It'll give you a look at the realities of the decline your company causes. When it comes to the park cleanup, sure, we can work side-by-side as long as you're willing to do anything I'm doing."

"And what will you be doing?" she asked, sensing the need to be wary.

"Oh, it'll be down and dirty..." he threatened with a whole lot of innuendo.

He was trying to rattle her and was succeeding. But she wasn't sure if it was because she didn't know what he might throw at her, or if it was the instant image that flashed through her mind of getting down and dirty with him in a way that had nothing to do with park cleanup. A way that was totally inappropriate and not at all businesslike.

But she refused to let him see that he was having any impact on her composure whatsoever and said matter-of-factly, "I'm not afraid of getting my hands dirty."

He smiled. "Said like a true Camden," he taunted.

Lindie raised a defiant chin but that only made him grin before he went on. "When it comes to Thursday, though, what I do with the kids is time I spend with them. If you want to come around, figure out something you can contribute to them yourself."

"Such as?"

"Go with your strengths. If you're a math or science whiz, or great with essays and writing book reports, you could help out in the quiet room—homework gets done in there. There's an art center if you draw or paint or sculpt or any of that stuff. Sometimes there are girls' basketball or volleyball pickup games—"

His gaze went down her legs to her spiked heels and his smile turned appreciative before he looked back at her face. "You might have to invest in a pair of tennis shoes for that, though," he added as if he doubted she owned anything that everyday.

Then he motioned to the room they were in. "There're

usually kids in here looking for somebody to play chess or checkers or a board game. Or there's a kitchen—we have some budding chefs who might appreciate a few lessons in there. Or you can help make sandwiches and snacks. There's always plenty to do. But on Thursdays it's the kids I'll be with, so don't think you can horn in on that."

Still, if she was in the same place at the same time he was, she thought she could find the opportunity to talk to him.

Just as she was plotting, a woman approached them, apologized for interrupting and said, "Do you think at the break you could talk to Parker Cauzel, Sawyer? He has some bruises on his arm that he's trying hard to hide. I don't know if something happened at home or—"

That took all the amusement out of Sawyer Huffman and before Lindie even knew she was going to say it, she asked, "He could be being abused?"

"His dad had to file bankruptcy and close his sporting goods store last week," Sawyer informed the other woman. "I know things are rough for the family right now." Then, pointedly to Lindie, he added, "Emotions can run high when times get tough. Tempers flare. Welcome to the real world."

Lindie was hardly out of touch with the real world. Especially most recently when it had landed her in the emergency room.

But she wasn't going to get into that.

The other woman spared her from saying anything by going on. "I heard from some of the other kids that Parker has had a few scuffles on the walks between school and here. If the bruises are from that, he needs a chat about not fighting. And if something worse is going on...? I know he likes you and I thought you might be able to talk to him to figure out if he just needs to vent some way other than with his fists or if we should get authorities involved."

"Sure, I'll talk to him. And while I have you here—is it true about the Murphys' mom?"

The woman's eyebrows rose in a helpless sort of shrug. "You know she's had problems making ends meet since her husband died. I guess she was doing something fraudulent on the internet and got caught. She pleaded guilty and will definitely go to jail so—with dad out of the picture, too—the four girls are with Grandma now," the woman confirmed.

"Lucky they have Grandma."

The woman glanced at Lindie apologetically. "I hope I wasn't breaking up something important but I just had a minute. I'll leave you two alone."

Then she left and Sawyer took a deep breath before he looked at Lindie again. All traces of amusement were gone from that handsome face. "There you go," he said, like a lawyer who felt he'd proved his case.

She must have looked confused.

"Two examples right under your nose. The bankruptcy is a direct result of a small business not being able to compete since your store came in. And even the Murphys. Their dad died a little over a year ago, and with businesses going under or cutting back around here mom couldn't get a job to support the family. I know she tried to get hired on with Camdens but was told you were bringing your own computer people in. I guess she went another route—one more side effect of 'Camden prosperity.'"

And by volunteering here Lindie was going to end up meeting the people harmed by those side effects.

Sawyer Huffman had no idea just how susceptible she was to that kind of thing.

I'm just going to have to be strong, she told herself.

"On second thought," he said, "maybe it isn't a good idea to have you coming around here even as a volunteer."

But if she didn't she knew she wasn't going to get anywhere near him.

"No one needs to know who I am. I won't give my last name. Or I'll use a different one if I need to," she said in a hurry, trying to maintain the ground she thought she'd gained.

He didn't answer immediately; instead he stared at her for a long moment as if weighing something.

Then he said, "Knockout or not, if I didn't know exactly who you are I doubt anyone else will recognize you, so I suppose it might be okay if you keep your identity under wraps. But you'd better tone it down some— there're not a lot of silk and six-hundred-dollar shoes being worn in this part of town."

The shoes had cost her eight hundred and just the fact that he realized they were expensive made her feel ashamed of that fact.

But again she wouldn't let him see it. She tilted her chin defiantly. "That's fine. I'm really not a prima donna."

"Yeah, I'll bet you've spent a lot of time in the trenches," he countered with biting sarcasm. "I guess we'll see, won't we?"

The challenge was back again and that, too, had an edge that made her think she was really in for it.

But nothing was going to make her back down so she

merely said, "When will you be handing out flyers tomorrow?"

"After work. Probably around six. If, once you think about things, you still want in, I'll meet you in the parking lot out front."

"I'll be here," she said.

There was skepticism in the wry half smile that quirked up one side of his sexy mouth, but he didn't say anything except, "I have to get back. You can find your way out?"

"I can."

He nodded his head, slowly, his crystal-blue eyes steady on her face.

Then, without saying goodbye, he went around her toward the chess tables, calling into the group, "Parker! How about a game to keep you sharp while you wait to play your next round?"

"Yeah? You think you can handle it?" a boy who looked to be about twelve or thirteen called back.

"Guess we'll see, won't we?" Sawyer answered, not giving Lindie as much as a backward glance.

And leaving her wondering if she'd just bitten off more than she could chew both with the man and the situation.

Chapter Two

"I won't let it happen, Candy. Sam is my son and he isn't moving to Vermont. I don't care if Harmon's practice here is hurting or that he wants to move closer to his family. *Sam's* family lives here and it's more important for the four-year-old to be with *his* family than for the thirty-four-year-old!"

Sawyer had been trying not to raise his voice as he spoke to his ex-girlfriend on the phone on Tuesday but he'd lost the battle.

"Maybe you should talk to Harmon," Candy Ferguson responded as if she were only partially involved.

"Maybe *you* should talk to Harmon! I know you don't want to move out of state. You've *never* wanted to move out of state. You gave up a college scholarship and used loans to pay your tuition rather than go away just for four years. Now this guy snaps his fingers and says he wants to move, so you're willing to do it? No way! Try standing up for yourself!"

"Vermont is nice…" was the wishy-washy answer to that.

They had been going round and round this issue for the past half hour and, so far, Sawyer hadn't gotten anywhere. He was fed up and pulled out what he hoped was his ace in the hole. "I've already talked to Sean." Sean was his younger brother and his attorney. "If I have to go to court, I will. If you don't have the guts to tell Harmon that you don't want to move, then feel free to make me the bad guy and use that as your out. But one way or another, I won't sit idly by and have you and *Harmon* take my son across the country to live."

He hung up without saying goodbye. Frustrated, angry, worried. And cursing himself for the choices he'd made in the women in his life.

"You're falling for it, too, *Harmon*," he muttered as if his ex's husband could hear. "I'm betting that she's letting you think she's okay with moving when she really isn't. Then she'll get there and be unhappy and blame you. But you're not taking my kid along for that ride!"

Sawyer was sitting behind the desk in his office. His door was closed for privacy so—knowing no one who worked for him could see—he dropped his head forward and reached back to try to rub the tension out of his neck.

It was bad enough to have his son living with another man half the time, to have Sam following some other guy's rules—because, of course, Candy wasn't going to be the boss. But at least Sawyer still had plenty of his own time with his son. Sawyer could be at T-ball games and school conferences and programs. Sawyer could pick Sam up from school. Sawyer could get to him in the blink of an eye if Sam was sick or hurt. He could *be there* for him.

If Sam was in Vermont, Sawyer would be relegated to phone and video calls, and he'd only actually be with his son a few times a year. And there was no way he wouldn't fight to keep that from happening.

The trouble was that he wasn't altogether sure it was a battle he would win.

Being part of Sam's life had been an uphill battle for a while now. Things had gone smoothly enough at the beginning. Candy hadn't known she was pregnant when their relationship had ended, but had told him as soon as she'd found out. She'd declined his suggestion of marriage but had agreed to let him have an active role as Sam's father. Or, at least, she'd conceded to it. He could never be too sure with her—or with any of the women who had passed through his adult life—whether agreement meant they were genuinely on board or just that they were going along against their will and not letting it show.

Either way, Candy had consented to letting him share custody, and even to naming Sam after Sawyer's father. Then she'd also accepted Sawyer's request for equal time with Sam, along with the ample child support he'd offered her.

It was only when Harmon had come on the scene two years ago that problems had started.

Sawyer's visitation with Sam had mysteriously gotten harder to schedule. Sawyer had stopped being included in decisions about Sam and was no longer informed about whatever was going on in Sam's life. He hadn't even been invited to Sam's last birthday party, and now Sawyer had to rely on the four-year-old to tell him most things, which, more often than not, resulted in only hearing about it after the fact.

But even though the problems started with Harmon, Sawyer couldn't be sure the other man was actually to blame.

He'd learned the hard way that just because Candy *seemed* okay with something, it didn't mean she was. That under the surface things could be simmering that he was completely unaware of, things that would flare up when he least expected it.

Did Candy really want to move to Vermont or was she not telling Harmon she didn't?

Was Harmon calling the shots with Sam, with Sawyer's visitation and participation in his son's life, or was Candy merely using him as an excuse to make Sam's upbringing go the way *she* wanted it?

Was it possible that Candy hadn't been so okay with sharing custody of Sam these past four years and moving to Vermont was her passive-aggressive way of cutting Sawyer out of his life?

Sawyer didn't know.

And he sure as hell couldn't say he was any good at deciphering what was really going on with her.

At the start, when Candy was being so agreeable to everything about Sam, Sawyer had taken into consideration that she was the primary caregiver, so he'd agreed to Candy being Sam's custodial parent.

Now, as the custodial parent, if she petitioned the court for relocation, a judge would most likely grant the relocation petition.

Besides Candy being the custodial parent, Sawyer's brother had said that the court would consider the fact that Sawyer often had to travel for work while Candy was a stay-at-home mom whose livelihood depended on her husband's income—an income that could be improved if Harmon took over his father's practice in Vermont instead of maintaining his own failing practice in Wheatley.

And off Sam would go to Vermont.

So Sawyer didn't want to go to court. But he might not have a choice. Because even though he thought it was possible that Candy honestly didn't want to move, he also didn't hold out much hope that she would openly admit it to her husband.

When it came to the women in his life, he'd definitely had a pattern. On the surface they'd all been agreeable, considerate, seemingly selfless women he'd thought were perfect partners. The kind of perfect partner his mom had been for his dad for the past four decades.

But instead of finding happily-ever-after the way his parents had, Sawyer had ended up accused and found guilty of relationship crimes he hadn't even known he was committing. As a result, his marriage and what he'd thought was a relationship headed for marriage with Candy had been dead in the water before he'd even realized anything was wrong.

And now his relationship with Sam could be on the line, unless he could rely on a woman speaking up—a woman he already knew was unlikely to do that.

He tapped his fingers on his desktop agitatedly.

He loved that kid more than he loved breathing. He couldn't lose him to Harmon and Vermont.

"Dammit!" he said under his breath, clenching his hands into two fists to stop the tapping.

A knock on his office door caused him to sit straighter and call a "Come in" as if nothing was bothering him.

His executive assistant poked her graying head through

the door. "The day is done. I just wanted to tell you that the fliers for the Wheatley park project are on my desk waiting for you, and to say good-night."

"Thanks, Marybeth. Have a nice night."

"You, too," the sixty-one-year-old answered before retreating and closing the door.

Sawyer checked the time and discovered it was nearly five-thirty. He needed to head for Wheatley.

He pushed his chair back and stood, shrugging out of his tan suit coat, taking off his tie, then unfastening the top button of his ecru shirt and rolling his long sleeves to his elbows.

Casual got a better reception in Wheatley.

In Wheatley where Lindie Camden was supposed to meet him.

If she showed.

Just the thought that she might helped to take his mind off his problems. And made him smile a little.

Lindie Camden.

Now *that* was an impressive ambassador to send to get on his good side!

The Camdens kept a relatively low profile but pictures of them cropped up here and there. Sawyer never paid enough attention to know who was who, but they did all bear a resemblance to each other—enough for him to have a general image of dark hair, fine features and blue eyes that were apparently considered so remarkable that the local media called them the Camden Blue Eyes—as if no one else in the world owned a pair.

To have the unusual request for an appointment followed by the appearance of a very un-Wheatley-looking woman in the community center's rec room hadn't made it a huge leap to suspect that that woman was the same one who had called. Lindie Camden.

When she'd turned around he'd seen that she'd had plenty to go along with those eyes that were, he had to admit, remarkable.

Lush, shiny, coffee-bean-colored hair down to the middle of her back. Skin like alabaster. High, well-defined cheekbones. Long, thick eyelashes. And full, sexy lips.

All together with well-shaped legs, a rear end the skirt she'd been wearing hugged to perfection, the temptation of just-the-right-size breasts peeking from behind silk folds, he could imagine treaties being signed between warring factions just because she asked.

Or at least he'd imagined it until she'd said she wanted to hire him. Then he'd reminded himself that he represented one side of those warring factions and that no matter how breathtaking the woman, he wasn't surrendering.

Take on Camden Incorporated as a client? Not a chance!

But he *had* seen another opportunity. An opportunity to open those big baby blues of hers to some of the damage her family's stores did.

If, in the process, he also found the opportunity to get her pretty little hands dirty cleaning up the mess left behind? There was just enough orneriness in him to get a kick out of the possibility of that.

Grabbing his discarded coat and tie, he took them with him as he went out of his office. A few of the people who worked for him were still there, wrapping things up for the day. After exchanging some small talk and goodnights, he picked up the fliers from Marybeth's desk and handed over locking-up duties to his office manager.

But Lindie Camden stayed on his mind.

Would her hair be down again today? he wondered. What would she be wearing? Surely not a skirt as tight as yesterday's or heels as high.

Not that it would matter. The woman could walk around barefoot, in rags, and still be gorgeous.

Had the Camdens thought that sending someone who looked the way she did would make him more apt to cave?

It seemed impossible for her looks not to be part of the plan. They'd probably thought to blind him with her beauty so he'd be putty in their hands.

Well, it wasn't going to work. A pretty face was not going to derail him professionally or get him to turn his back on what he believed in or on the people and businesses he was glad to represent.

And it wasn't going to get to him personally, either, he thought as he got into his SUV and found himself feeling his jaw the way he might have if he were about to go on a date; testing to see if he should take his emergency electric razor out of the glove compartment for a second shave today.

There was a little stubble and, yeah, if this *was* a date, he probably would have used the razor.

But this wasn't a date so he didn't.

No matter how attractive she was, he wouldn't touch a Camden with a ten-foot pole, he thought as he merged into highway traffic in the direction of Wheatley. And not only out of loyalty to his family—although that was certainly a factor. Not even if he wasn't in a mess over Sam that drove home his need to reassess why things always went so wrong with his choices in women.

On top of both of those things, Lindie Camden was also his business enemy and that was automatically a roadblock. Roadblocks were huge challenges and challenges in his personal relationships were things he tried to avoid. Things that certainly didn't *improve* relationships.

No matter what, he liked things in his personal life to be smooth sailing. He wanted a woman he was completely compatible with. A relationship that was pleasant and harmonious. Like his parents had. He was sure wanting that wasn't where he'd gone wrong in the past and he wasn't changing it.

And there was no chance that any of that could come about with a woman he was at odds with from the get-go. Especially one who was likely spoiled and pampered and accustomed to getting her own way about everything. A woman who probably didn't know the meaning of the word *compromise*.

So, thanks but no thanks all the way around, Lindie Camden!

The most he was going to indulge himself in was rubbing her nose in what her stores left behind. In getting her hands dirty cleaning up some of it.

Other than that, this whole thing was going to be nothing more than a small amusement until she turned tail and ran back to the family in defeat.

In the meantime he'd just take in the view as a bonus and use his time with her to make his point. To show the almighty Camdens why they deserved to have things made difficult for them. And not only because there was the stain of the earlier Camdens' underhanded dealings on their record.

Oh, yeah, Lindie Camden was in for it. He'd make sure of that. Regardless of how hot she was.

And the fact that when he reached the first stoplight in Wheatley, he took his shaver out of the glove box to run over his face, after all? That didn't mean anything except that he wanted to make a good impression on the people he encountered tonight in the process of handing out fliers.

It wasn't because he was sprucing up to see Lindie Camden again.

Lindie was in her car in the parking lot of the Wheatley Community Center at five minutes before six o'clock on Tuesday night. She was watching every car that pulled in until she could see if the driver was Sawyer Huffman.

And wondering why it was that she'd been so eager for this all day long. Why it was that every car made her hopes rise and her pulse race. Why it was that she deflated into disappointment each time the driver proved not to be him.

She was just eager to get this deal done, she told herself. To get Sawyer on board with Camden Inc. so he stopped making things difficult. To put him in line for a nice fat payday to make up for the past. And then she could go on with her life.

It didn't have anything to do with the image of the man himself that had been popping into her mind since she'd seen him here yesterday. All big and tall and broad-shouldered and hella-handsome—

No, no, no, that didn't have anything to do with it.

And it also wasn't the reason she'd left work an hour early today, gone home and changed from business clothes into her favorite navy blue butt-hugging pants and the tailored white blouse that followed every curve so closely the buttons barely kept from gapping.

Or the reason she'd untwisted her hair from its French knot, brushed it and left it loose again.

Or the reason she'd refreshed her blush and mascara

and applied the new sassy-rose lip gloss she'd just bought on Saturday.

It *had* been with him in mind that she'd chosen her shoes, though. Two-inch wedge sandals bought at a bargain price and far more conservative than the spiked heels she'd worn on Monday.

The fact that they also showed her just-pedicured toes was purely coincidental.

Sawyer was driving a big white SUV when she finally spotted him pulling into the lot.

The knight on the white charger—that's probably how he sees himself, she thought, given that he seemed to have the impression that Camden Inc. was a big, bad evil he was trying to rescue people from.

Lindie hid her purse under her passenger seat and got out, locking the doors on her metallic-gray sedan and putting her keys in her pants' pocket.

He parked in the spot next to her, taking off sunglasses that made him all the more rakish-looking and hooking them on his visor before joining her.

Not that the removal of the sunglasses muted any of his appeal. The man was simply fantastic-looking.

But that didn't make any difference. Even if he had warts and boils she would still have had the same job to do and she'd do it the exact same way.

"You're here," he greeted as he closed and locked his car door.

"I said I would be."

"I thought you'd find an excuse not to be."

"Fooled you," she said victoriously. "Here I am. Ready to walk the streets."

Oh, that hadn't sounded good.

And he'd caught it because it made him grin before

he said, "I'm trying really hard not to make an inappropriate joke right now."

"I appreciate that," she said, curious about exactly what the joke might be. But she was here for business not for pleasure, so she opted to get to it. "Where do we start?" she asked enthusiastically.

"This way," he said, pointing with that dimpled chin of his to the street that ran in front of the center and heading there.

"This is the park we'll be cleaning up—right next door," he informed her as they took a left turn onto the sidewalk. "City resources are going into an upscale version near your store on the other side of town and this one has been left to rot."

"It definitely needs work," Lindie commented as she took in the sight of rundown, damaged picnic tables and play equipment, of trees that needed trimming, of the signs of overall neglect.

Beyond the park they began to go up and down streets lined with small frame houses, heading for front doors to leave the fliers he was carrying.

While Lindie could see that it had been a nice middle-class area once upon a time, now there were only a few houses that were well-kept. More often than not yards were either overtaken by weeds or totally bare. When it came to the houses themselves, too many had chipped and peeling paint or siding, missing shutters and shingles or other signs of disrepair.

"It costs money to water lawns. To fertilize grass and flowers and to kill weeds. To paint and fix things when they age or weather takes a toll," Sawyer said when he noticed her avoiding the brown branches of a dead hedge to one side of a small porch. "And it takes time that a lot of people had when it was a ten-minute drive to and from work, but don't have now that it's an hour or more commute every day."

Lindie didn't comment, especially when they passed a house that was obviously vacant and had a foreclosure notice in the front window. But she did feel the weight on her conscience and in response she picked up some toys dropped in the yard of the next house and left them neatly stacked at the door as Sawyer slid the flyer into a grate on a screen torn away from the frame.

There was an elderly man working on the engine of an equally elderly truck at the next house. Sawyer said hello and approached him with the fliers.

"Think you could hold this for me for a minute?" the elderly man asked.

Sawyer passed the fliers to Lindie so he could assist with something in the engine. As she stood there waiting it occurred to her that all of the vehicles parked in driveways and at the curbs were dated. That there wasn't a new car anywhere to be seen.

"Okay, I can take it from here," the old man said a moment later, handing Sawyer a rag to wipe his hands on and glancing at the flier he accepted from Lindie.

"Glad somebody's doin' something with that park," the man said. "It's turning into another eyesore around here and we don't need any more of those."

"Maybe you can come down and help out," Sawyer suggested encouragingly.

"Maybe," the man allowed as Sawyer said they'd let him get back to his work.

He took the fliers from Lindie so they could move on.

Block after block, they encountered more of the same downtrodden homes and people. Several residents either complained about the decay and neglect or wearily committed to helping and voiced their hope that something would improve the area.

Lindie took it all in, continuing her own minor aid by picking up a bicycle or a newspaper here and there to bring up to the house it belonged to, by righting an overturned lawn chair, by doing whatever small thing she could when she encountered it.

Fences were also casualties at many houses and a humorously ferocious Yorkshire terrier leashed to a post let them know he would rather have been free to run around the yard that could no longer contain him—or at least that was Sawyer's interpretation of the yipping that greeted them.

Worse than the houses whose owners were clearly having trouble maintaining them was the small shopping center they came to late in the evening. Darkness was just beginning to fall and they'd come almost full circle when Sawyer stopped to point it out.

The shopping center was downhill from where they stood so they could look out over the entire area. There were four buildings with multiple storefronts in each one, all of them vacant. Windows were broken in or boarded up. Graffiti, litter, cracked pavement and the signs of general decay made the whole thing an ugly blot on the landscape. Worse, it was a gathering spot for some unsavory-looking teenagers currently loitering there.

"This place is the most direct result of your store," Sawyer said. "Before there was a Camden Superstore there were tenants in every one of those storefronts. Now they've all gone broke or moved. We've requested that the Urban Renewal Authority come in and make it a revitalization project but so far they haven't agreed and this is what the area is left with."

There was no denying how bad it was, so Lindie didn't try. And despite the guilt she felt, she said, "It isn't our goal to do damage to any community. We always go into an area conscientiously and we do everything we can not to cause problems. We make offers to small businesses to buy them out but if they refuse and then can't compete and go broke, or if they accept and the buildings that housed them get abandoned—"

"It ends up like this," he concluded, not letting her off the hook. "And it lowers the value of every piece of property around it."

"We can't go in and buy every house that might decrease in value because another part of town booms and theirs busts," she argued. But even though she knew the words were true, they didn't make her feel any less terrible about what she was seeing tonight.

"No. But, for instance, you could have bought those buildings down there and offered the businesses in them rents reduced enough to let them survive. You could have introduced a program to bring in businesses and shops that offered products or services that didn't have to compete with Camden Superstores. You could have offered existing business owners other avenues—retraining or something that kept their doors open *somehow*. That kept this area alive. Instead it's just decimated and all because of you."

"Those are suggestions I can make! Things I can push for in the future—"

"Uh-huh. And *maybe* you'll come through. Or maybe, if you shut me up, you don't have to bother. That is why I'll never take you on as a client. It's why I won't stop warning communities that this is what can happen when you come in. Why not only won't I stop trying to protect areas and residents from the residual havoc you wreak but why I sure as hell won't work *for* you and end up a part of the problem!"

"If you worked for us maybe you could be the one to push us to take your suggestions."

"Sure," he said, his tone making it clear he wasn't buying that for a minute.

Lindie didn't give up. "Maybe you could keep on top of the problems when they develop, before they get to this point, and bring them to our attention."

"Oh, very slick," he said as they moved on, returning to the community center parking lot. "And once I'm on your payroll it would mean my job if I made a stink and refused to spout the company line. Again—not a chance," he repeated as they reached the driver's side of her car and stopped.

"Did this *all* come from my uncle winning my aunt from your father?" Lindie asked, feeling frustrated with his hardline stance.

"*Winning* implies a fair fight," he said, arching an eyebrow as he leaned against the side of his SUV, settling in to focus on her. "Camdens don't fight fair."

"But we do!"

He ignored that claim and instead answered her question. "No, this doesn't *all* come from what went on between my father and your uncle. It started there—certainly I grew up hearing that story more than once. Then there were a couple of things that added to it."

"Like what?"

"Like the Camden Superstore that went into Dunhaven when I was in middle school. My dad was in construction. He worked all over and he'd seen what happened in the wake of your stores. He knew what we were in for. So by the time I was ready to go to high school my folks decided they'd better sell the house I'd grown up in and get out while the getting was good."

"Part of Dunhaven ended up like this side of Wheatley?"

"Yeah, it did," he said as if wondering how she could not know that.

"So you and your parents—"

"And my younger brother, moved," he went on. "My parents had to take a loss on the house to sell it. I ended up having to enter a different school district and leave behind all my friends."

"That didn't make you happy," Lindie commented, interpreting his tone.

"No, that did *not* make me happy. And when I went back to visit those friends I saw this." He motioned to what she'd now had her eyes opened to.

"The last time I went back—for a Friday-night visit in the summer," he continued, "my old friends were bashing in windows for entertainment. The movie theater had closed. They didn't have anything else to do. The building they were vandalizing was a tire store in an area of town that had been doing okay when I moved. But thanks to Camden Superstore's automotive department it had eventually gone under and so had my friend's father—he'd managed it. My friend had a lot of pent-up anger about it and that was how he let it out. It was the last time my parents let me go back to visit, but I heard over the transom that that particular friend kept to that path. He got into more and more trouble and ended up in jail."

"And you blame us," Lindie attested.

"I can tell you firsthand that he wasn't on the road to prison before your store came in and ruined his old man…" He left the rest of the answer to her.

"Then, in college, H. J. Camden came up in a couple of my business courses," Sawyer went on. "I'll grant you that it wasn't always negative—he is quite a success story and more than one of my business professors admired the hell out of him. But he also came up on a list of modern-day robber barons."

Lindie had heard that title applied to her great-grandfather before but it still caused her to flinch. "And *that* was what you paid attention to," she concluded.

"Like I said, I grew up on the story of a Camden's ruthlessness. So, yeah, I paid a lot of attention to that side of things."

"And that was when you declared war on all Camdens?"

He motioned with one hand to all that was around them. "I had good reasons *not* to admire you all. Nothing personal," he added.

"Right," Lindie said with a tone full of sarcasm, goading him. "Because *personally* you admire me."

He smiled a sly half smile and shrugged, leaving her unsure exactly what that meant. It did seem as if he might at least be admiring the way she looked, though, because his cool blue eyes never veered to take in anything else.

Then he said, "Are you and the corporation the same thing? Isn't there anything about you that isn't business to *be* admired?"

"There's a lot about me that isn't business." Why was this starting to sound a little flirty?

"Like what?" he asked. "Are you married? Because there's no ring. Kids?"

"No, I'm not married."

"Ever been?"

"No. So I also don't have any kids."

"You can have one without the other," he informed her as if letting her in on a secret.

"Well, I haven't."

"So what is there about you that isn't business?" he challenged.

"I have a nephew—Carter—who I love to death. And there's a new baby in the family—Immy—that my cousin's about-to-be wife inherited. I love babysitting for her, too. And there's my family. And I have four dogs."

"*Four?* Let me guess, some snobby kind of show dogs?"

"Actually, they're four rescue mutts that were hard to place. And whenever there's a need for a temporary foster home for dogs requiring special care until they can be adopted, I take those, too." Because all the local animal shelters knew she was a soft touch.

"You realize that when your stores do what they've done to places like Wheatley and the economy suffers, so do pets. If people are struggling to feed their kids, they certainly can't feed their dogs and those dogs end up needing to be rescued."

"Oh, you just never miss an opening, do you?" she lamented, feeling more weight on her conscience.

But this time, rather than tell her she deserved it, he grinned and said somewhat sheepishly, "One too many jabs?"

"If I cry uncle will you stop?"

"Maybe for now."

"Uncle!" she said.

That made him grin again. "Okay. You *did* do your

own little cleanup tonight along the way, I'll give you that."

Lindie made a face, knowing that picking up a bicycle here or a newspaper there was inconsequential and that nothing had really been solved tonight. Not for Wheatley and not for her goal of winning over and compensating Sawyer Huffman.

Yet, somehow, even given all that, she'd enjoyed the long walk and talking to Sawyer in spite of everything else.

"So Thursday..." she said. "What time do you come here?"

"I'm with the kids on Thursdays," he warned, reminding her that he was unavailable.

"I'll still be here," she insisted. After seeing more of Wheatley she felt a need to do something. Coming to the center wasn't only about finding an excuse to get to him anymore.

"I end my work schedule at two-thirty on Thursdays so I can get here by three, about the time the kids start showing up after school."

"I'll be here at three, then," she said.

He didn't say anything but this time it didn't look as if he doubted her the way he had yesterday.

Instead, sounding as if he was admitting something reluctantly, he said, "I'm glad you came tonight." He smiled mischievously. "Even if I did give you a hard time, it was better than walking the streets alone."

Lindie laughed at his gentle gibe over her verbal gaffe at the start of the evening. "You just couldn't let it go completely."

"I couldn't," he confessed. "But that was so much tamer than anything else I could have said."

He pushed off his SUV and reached around her to open her door for her, waiting with it open as she got in behind the wheel.

"I'll see you Thursday," she repeated.

For some reason he smiled as if he was glad to hear it this time. But all he said was "Drive safe," before he closed her door.

Lindie started her engine and drove off. As she did she hated to admit to herself that—in spite of how it had made her feel to see the damage that her family had caused—she'd been on dates that she'd enjoyed less than her time with Sawyer Huffman tonight.

But as soon as she realized that, she decided to take it as a caution.

The man *really* didn't like Camdens and could easily have a hidden agenda when it came to one of them.

And since Lindie was already no stranger to men with hidden agendas that ended up hurting her, she knew very well to watch out.

Chapter Three

"If I lived in that part of Wheatley I'd hate us, too," Lindie concluded.

It was lunchtime on Thursday. Lindie was in her office on the top floor of the Camden Building that housed the offices for all ten of the Camden grandchildren. But the door was closed and no one was in on that particular lunch but Lindie and her grandmother.

Georgianna Camden—who everyone called GiGi— had brought beautiful Cobb salads for Lindie and herself to eat so that Lindie could report on her first two encounters with Sawyer Huffman.

As matriarch of the Camden family, GiGi had been the one to read the journals kept by the late H. J. Camden—founder of all of the Camden enterprises, great-grandfather to Lindie, her brothers, sisters and cousins, and father-in-law to GiGi.

As much as all of the current Camdens wished it wasn't true, having H.J. on a list of modern-day robber barons was not unfounded.

Rumors and accusations had always swirled around H.J.; his son Hank, who was GiGi's husband; and Hank and GiGi's sons, Howard and Mitchum. Through the years various people had claimed their business practices were dirty, unscrupulous, underhanded, ruthless and all-round heinous. The men themselves had denied any wrongdoing. And since they'd been loving, caring husbands, fathers and grandfathers, those denials were believed within the family.

Until H.J.'s journals had been discovered at the Camden ranch in Northbridge, Montana.

Reading the journals had proved to GiGi that most of the accusations against the men that all of the current Camdens had loved and respected were actually true. As a result the current Camdens were attempting to seek out some of the people who had taken the brunt of former Camdens' misdeeds and trying to make it up to them directly or through remaining family members.

Settling business grudges was hard enough. Personal grudges, as with the Huffmans, were even tougher. And what had occurred for personal reasons now had business consequences for the Camdens.

"It's just awful, GiGi," Lindie went on. "Seeing firsthand how, because of us, people have lost their livelihoods. How perfectly nice homes are now run-down. How hard times are causing domestic violence and crime and families coming apart at the seams and—"

"Okay, okay, slow down, Lindie," her grandmother interrupted. "You're getting carried away again. I know you think you have to cure all the ills in the world but you're supposed to be working on trying to curb some of that, remember?"

"I know. I know," Lindie said. "But—"

"No buts."

"But there are kids and—"

"No buts!" GiGi raised her voice. "You *need* to stop this! To toughen up. We've caused problems. We'll do what we can about them. We'll do whatever it takes to avoid them in the future. But that's not what you're supposed to be looking at now and so far that's all you've talked about. We've finished with lunch and I still haven't heard anything about Sawyer Huffman. The situation with *him* is what we need you to work on now."

Lindie took a deep breath and exhaled, knowing her grandmother was right; that she did need to get control of her runaway compulsion to save everyone.

"It's one thing to be sensitive," her grandmother went on lecturing. "To care as much as you about…well, everything. We're all proud of that in you. But you can't take care of everything or everyone. There has to be limits and you still have to learn when and where to set them. So for right now, let's just concentrate on Sawyer Huffman."

Sawyer Huffman with those pale, crystal-clear blue eyes shot through with silver rays…

She might not have said much about him yet but her grandmother didn't need to be worried that she wasn't concentrating on him. Yes, her sense of responsibility and guilt was in overdrive again when it came to Wheatley, but not even that had kept her from thinking far, far, far too much about Sawyer Huffman.

Although she had to admit that her thoughts were less on the situation than on the man himself. The image of that sculpted face…that dented chin. The way his lips quirked just so when he smiled. Those broad shoulders and big, big hands and arms he liked to cross over that impressive chest…

Even the deep, whiskey tone of his voice had gotten to her so much she'd been having trouble *not* thinking about him. And she'd tried. Boy, had she tried!

She just hadn't succeeded.

"He's pretty unwavering about us and not taking us on as clients," Lindie told her grandmother, using business to defuse some of those rampant thoughts about Sawyer Huffman. "He's nice enough about it. He's not hostile and so far I haven't seen signs that he bears too much of a grudge for what went on with his father. He mentioned that it was an influence on him but he hasn't said more than that."

"Yet."

"Right. Yet. But up to now all I've seen is that he's very matter-of-fact about how much he likes the role he's carved out for himself as our enemy. It's a role he thinks needs to be filled on behalf of places like Wheatley and its residents, and I'm not sure how—or *if*—I can get him to change anything. He doesn't even seem to care about the money he could make from us. I don't think it even tempts him, so I'm not quite sure what will."

"These things always look impossible at the start," GiGi insisted. "Especially this one because Samuel Huffman and Huffman Construction rebounded so well after what your uncle Howard did that I couldn't find any way that we could make anything up to him directly. That's why you have to really get to know his son. That will help you find a way in. Then you'll be able to figure out what we can do in the form of restitution for what happened in the past and, hopefully, get us on the path to better relations for the future. This project is tailor-made for you, Lindie. You like to fix everyone's problems and I think this is a good avenue for that. You just can't let yourself be pulled in other directions. Put the problems of Wheatley, its economy and the people in it on hold for the time being and just find a way to fix things with Sawyer Huffman first. Tunnel vision—you have *got* to develop some!"

Lindie nodded, understanding what her grandmother was saying. Agreeing with it. She just wasn't altogether sure she was capable of ignoring so many other problems to deal only with the task she'd been given.

But there was a lot riding on this particular mission beyond making amends. Huffman Consulting turned every proposed new store into a political hotbed to keep it from happening. The situation needed to be neutralized somehow and it was her job to do that.

"I'm volunteering this afternoon at the Wheatley Community Center so I can see him again," she said, wondering after the words were out why that didn't sound as businesslike as it should.

"Okay, but remember that *he's* your goal. Don't get sucked into other things," GiGi warned, apparently not hearing what Lindie had heard in her own words.

"I won't," she promised as her grandmother stood to leave.

"Keep me posted," the elderly woman said by way of a goodbye.

"I will," Lindie assured her.

Once she was alone in her office she chastised herself for what she'd said.

Technically it was true that she was volunteering at

the center to see Sawyer again. But it wasn't as if seeing him again was for pleasure.

And yet...

Okay, she was looking forward to seeing him again, she admitted to herself. She didn't want to be, but she couldn't help it.

The guy was great-looking. He was intelligent. Interesting. He had a sense of humor.

And she was only human. If she'd met him at a party she would have hoped he'd ask for her number or ask her out.

But even if they'd met under those circumstances, even if there wasn't history between their families to start things off on the wrong foot, even if he wasn't her business foe, he still wasn't someone she would be looking at as a potential partner, she reminded herself.

At thirty she knew it would be naive and unrealistic to expect to meet eligible men who didn't have any romantic problems in their past at all. Sure, she'd never been married, didn't have any kids, and it would be nice to find someone in that same situation. Someone who'd had just a couple of serious relationships in their past to teach them a thing or two and leave them with valuable experience that wasn't baggage they'd never be able to leave behind.

So given that that requirement might narrow the field a little too much, she was okay with a past that included a divorce. She even tried to look on the bright side by acknowledging that while a divorce was a bigger deal than a long-term romance gone bad, she could still consider it evidence that the man could make a serious commitment, that he could get all the way to the altar.

What she didn't want was a man who had a child.

She loved kids. She wanted kids. But she really wanted her kids to be the only kids her husband had. She really didn't want someone who was pulled in two directions— toward the family he had with her and the family he'd started with someone else.

At thirty she knew that also narrowed the field, but that was a narrowing she was willing to accept to have a man without lifelong complications from his past.

And Sawyer Huffman had a child.

To her that put an immediate kibosh on the slightest idea of anything romantic between them, even if there weren't the obstacles of family history and business.

It was just that the man also had a lot to offer at a glance…

Those looks.

That confident, brash, strong personality tempered with humor and what appeared to be an even temper.

That sexiness that just seemed to be natural to him without him putting any effort into it.

And that whole fighting-for-the-underdog determination that really hit home for her.

That was a whole lot that was impossible to ignore and, yes, it did make her want to see him again.

But if she controlled anything, she vowed, it was going to be what she would only admit reluctantly might be an attraction to him.

Because there just wasn't anywhere for that to go. There just wasn't anywhere she wanted it to go. Anywhere she would let it go.

As far as she was concerned, Sawyer Huffman already had three strikes against him.

The bad history between their families, their professional conflicts and a child.

And that counted him out as a relationship prospect regardless of his appeal.

Because as determined as she was to get this job she'd been given done, she was even more determined about that!

Angel, Casey, Biz—who was really Elizabeth—and Clara. Lindie had repeated the names of the four Murphy sisters several times to remember which was which as she worked with them in the community center's kitchen that afternoon. Angel was the oldest at eleven, Casey was nine, Biz was eight and Clara was seven.

They were the four girls whose dad had died, whose mother had turned to computer crime to support them, who were now living with their grandmother while their mother went to jail.

When Lindie had arrived at the center she'd again said only that she was there to see Sawyer. But this time she was asked her name and when she gave it—only Lindie—the woman who introduced herself as Marie greeted her warmly and said, "Sawyer told us you might be coming to volunteer."

Marie had then cheerily explained that she was the volunteer coordinator and that it was her job to familiarize new volunteers with the center's layout and to put them to work.

A tour was the first order of business and as Lindie was shown the recreation room, she saw Sawyer in the distance at a chess table, playing chess with the boy—Parker Cauzel—who he'd been asked to talk to on Monday.

Sawyer appeared to be watching for her because he spotted her the minute she entered the rec room and waved. But that was the extent of their interaction. He stayed at the chess table and Marie kept Lindie occupied.

It made her wonder if he'd set up the whole thing to make sure she *didn't* get to him. And while that frustrated and concerned her since she was there expressly for the purpose of seeing him, it also disappointed her and struck a bit of a blow to her ego.

He'd warned her that he spent Thursdays with the kids and wouldn't be available to her. But she hadn't taken that too seriously.

Since she'd been so eager to get there today to see him, it was a little demoralizing to think that he hadn't been as eager to see her; that instead he might have arranged for her to be intercepted by someone else to keep her away from him.

In fact, it was more than a little demoralizing.

But with no choice except to go through the new-volunteer orientation with Marie, that's what Lindie did. When it came to deciding where her skills could be best used and she tried for the rec room, she was told that there were enough volunteers in the rec room today. Instead she was steered toward the kitchen where help was needed.

Still, making the best of the situation and hoping to connect with him later, Lindie had jumped in in the kitchen and accepted the assignment of making a snack using what was available—several boxes of graham crackers.

Since there were also the ingredients for frosting, Lindie made a suggestion and got the okay before she was left with the four Murphy girls to get to work.

"This was our favorite afterschool snack when I was little," she said as she taught the girls how to make a simple chocolate frosting. Then she and the two older Murphys spread the frosting on one side of graham crackers, handing them over to the younger girls to top with a second graham cracker and stack on plates.

As they worked it didn't take much for the girls to warm up to her—they were impressed with her hair and interested in how she twisted it in back and left curls to erupt out of the twist at her crown. They liked her simple twill slacks and the embroidery down the front of her blouse. They *loved* her shoes—ballet flats that were the same blue-black of her pants and had white polka dots all over them.

The longer they worked together, the more they interjected information about themselves, too, letting Lindie get to know them. She concluded that they were lovely, polite little girls trying to cover up the fact that their mother had done something wrong.

By the time they had several plates stacked with the graham cracker sandwiches, which the sisters were very impressed with, Lindie was beginning to feel like one of the girls.

"Do we bring these around to everyone now?" she asked, hoping it would get her nearer to Sawyer.

"Everybody knows to come in to see if there's something when they want to eat," Angel informed her just as Clara was motioning to Lindie to bend so she could whisper in her ear.

When Lindie did, the seven-year-old said, "Could I bring one home to my gramma? She likes chocolate but we couldn't buy any at the store yesterday because she had to buy so much other stuff for us to eat. We had to put her candy bars back when we didn't have enough money at the end."

And that was as much as it took to break Lindie's heart.

She had no idea what the center's policy was on sending food home. She'd used all the graham crackers available to arrive at the number of portions Marie had said she should have, and she couldn't risk that other kids there might go without if she wrapped even one up for Clara.

But during the tour she'd been shown the employee's lounge and where to put her purse. And she'd seen a vending machine there.

So, ruled only by her need to send something chocolate home with that child, she said, "I think we only have enough crackers for the kids here. But if you don't tell anyone, I know where I can get a candy bar for you to take home to your gramma."

Clara beamed with delight. "She likes the ones with nuts."

"It has to be just between you and me, though," Lindie warned, worried that she was stepping over some kind of boundary. "Do you have a backpack or somewhere we can kind of hide it?"

"A backpack, yeah," the little blond girl confirmed.

While the other sisters and more kids began to wander in to take the snacks, Lindie slipped away to the employee lounge, got money from her purse and went to the vending machine.

Since she was alone in the lounge—and thinking that she couldn't send Clara Murphy's grandmother a candy bar without sending treats for the girls, too—she ended up putting five candy bars into her pockets before a voice from behind her said, "Are you having a blood sugar crisis?"

She jumped.

Unlike her first visit to the center, this time she recognized the voice.

Sawyer.

She'd been so intent on what she was doing she hadn't heard him come in. Or step up to stand close behind her.

She turned around to face him, still wondering if he'd arranged for her not to get near him today. And if he had, what was he doing there now?

"Hi," she said, taking in the sight of him in what she assumed was the remainder of his work suit—grayish-blue slacks and a light blue shirt he wore with the collar button unfastened and the long sleeves rolled to mid-forearms.

Yep, still terrific-looking.

If only that could be toned down some.

"Is there a reason you're stuffing candy bars in your pockets?" he reiterated.

"The profits go to the center?" she said with a nod at the note taped to the machine.

It was a lame answer and he saw through it. "Try again?"

She told him what she was doing.

"That's not a good idea, Lindie," he said when she had. "Kids will work you, if you let them. And even if the candy really is for Gramma, kids also talk and you'll have this whole place wanting you to do the same thing for them. Plus once word gets out that you're a soft touch or kids think you're gullible you could be in line for—"

She knew he was right. She'd been in this situation before too many times to count. And yet... "Clara is seven. She isn't a mastermind manipulator. And all she wanted was one lousy chocolate-frosted graham cracker to take to her grandmother. My grandmother took me in—along with my brothers and sisters and cousins—when we didn't have anywhere else to go, too. Granted, money wasn't an issue, but I can't imagine how awful I would have felt if she'd had to sacrifice something she wanted to feed us. I felt bad enough about other things, it would have been even worse to know that. It's just a few stupid candy bars and I've already told Clara she can't say anything about it. But even if she does and I end up having to buy them for the whole place, then fine. But today Clara needs to take her gramma a treat and I'm going to make sure she can. Shoot me."

He shook that handsome head of his. Just when she thought he was going to tell her there were rules against this or something along those lines, he sighed and said, "I know the Murphy girls. I know that they're good kids and that none of them is diabetic or has allergies—because if you don't know those things, you could be causing real problems with treats like this. But because I know that with these particular kids it's probably okay... Come on, I'll play lookout while you give them to her. This once!"

The downside was just that it made her like *him* more, but Lindie only said, "Thanks," and then took him up on his offer by leading him to the kitchen where Clara was watching for her.

The little girl ran up to her expectantly and the three of them went to where the backpacks were kept. While Sawyer blocked them from view with his back to them, keeping an eye out for witnesses, Lindie passed the candy bars to the child to stash, wondering how this would look on a security camera if there had been one.

But there was just no way she could have lived with herself if she'd refused the child.

When the deed was done and Clara left them to return to the kitchen, Lindie again watched Sawyer shake his head at her. But what he said was "I have another game waiting for me. Try not to get yourself into more trouble, huh?"

He left her standing there, still with no idea if he was trying to avoid her deliberately.

And with nothing else to do but go on with her kitchen duties, Lindie went back to clean up and finish the afternoon.

At six o'clock the community center was turned over to adult education, art and fitness classes.

Rather than shoving kids out the door at the stroke of six, one person from the daytime schedule remained with them in the lobby to keep an eye on the children waiting to be picked up.

That night Sawyer was the person.

While Lindie still wasn't sure if he was open to it, his staying back finally gave her the chance to talk to him so she joined him.

"Get into any more mischief?" he asked as she sat with him on a bench.

"I don't think so. I did talk to Clara about not even telling her sisters what I'd done, about just giving the loot over to her grandmother on the sly and letting her grandmother take it from there."

"I hope that happens and Clara doesn't just down five candy bars herself—*on the sly*."

"I have faith in her," Lindie said, knowing that too many times in the past she'd said that same thing only to discover that her faith in someone had been unfounded.

But hopefully that wouldn't be the case here.

Sawyer nodded with a slow, we'll-see kind of air to it as he kept those keen blue eyes on her for a lengthy moment.

"Stuff will get to you here, Lindie. You have to be careful. There are a lot of hardships, a lot of need, a lot of sad things going on. But you can't just step in with a quick fix or a pocketful of candy bars every time. That can end up a disaster."

"So you just ignore it?"

"No. You ask questions. You try to find out if there might be a bigger problem that could have a better all-around solution or help that doesn't depend on you hitting the vending machine."

Lindie shot him a mock frown. "I thought I was to blame for everything and was *supposed* to make things right."

"Not like today," he said.

"Instead I should have turned it over to the Candy Bar Outreach program?"

"Instead you ask if there were other things Gramma couldn't afford at the grocery store—like milk or eggs or cereal or meat. You try to find out if there's enough to eat in general—healthy stuff. You might have found out that it wasn't only candy bars that Gramma couldn't swing. And if that's the case—or even if you just find out that things are a little too tight—you hand over the information to Marie who will talk to our social worker. Then the social worker will look into it to see if maybe food stamps would help ease some of the burden. What you heard today could have been a clue to a much bigger problem than Gramma not getting her sugar fix."

"Oh," Lindie said, knowing that once again she should have proceeded with some caution.

"It's better if you don't just rush in," he said as if he'd heard her thoughts. "The social worker here is great. She's amazingly diplomatic and she knows how to approach these things so nobody ends up feeling like their toes have been stepped on, or like their kids have aired dirty laundry. They can get the help they need and keep their pride intact."

Lindie flinched. "You think I offended Gramma?"

"Again, I know these girls and I've met Gramma and she's a really nice, down-to-earth, levelheaded lady, so I know this isn't going to cause problems at home and she'll probably just eat the candy. And I already talked to Marie, told her it might be good to have the social worker do an interview to see if Gramma needs some help with the expenses of four kids added to her budget. But from here on—"

"I'll watch myself," Lindie swore, thinking that this was the second time today she'd had to make that vow when it came to this place.

Sawyer accepted it easier than her grandmother had, though, because he seemed to relax his posture, stretching both arms along the top of the bench and looking at her as if he was getting his first glance of the day.

Then, in a more conversational vein, he said, "So, what is it you do for the family business if you aren't their assassin—which, by the way, I'm still not quite convinced of since you're hanging around. You aren't just hoping for the chance to make toast of me tonight, after all, are you?"

"Is that why I wasn't assigned the rec room? You fear for your life?" she countered.

His expression showed some confusion. "I don't have

anything to do with where volunteers are sent for the day."

So, possibly, it hadn't been a conspiracy?

He wasn't trying to get away from her now—or even trying to persuade her to leave. Instead he was chatting with her. Lindie decided to give him the benefit of the doubt and drop her suspicions.

"I have a degree in communications." She answered his question simply. "So I oversee our public relations. And sometimes, if it's absolutely necessary for someone in the family to speak out, I'm our spokesperson."

"How come I haven't seen you before this, then? Because believe me, I would have remembered."

The appreciation in the way he was looking at her convinced her that was true. But she tried not to take it to heart. "I've been our spokesperson several times in my eight years on the job but it's always been to announce positive things, so they probably didn't interest you enough to pay attention."

He was paying attention to her now, though. Close attention. "I know Camden Inc. is family owned and operated," he said. "So how does that work? What's the hierarchy? Who's the boss?"

"The titles are really just formalities. Camden Inc. was left to H.J.'s ten great-grandchildren. The way he set it up, we run it—we're the board of directors—and we each have one vote in everything so no one carries more clout than anyone else."

"And that works?" Sawyer asked skeptically.

"It does for us. To be honest, it's the way we were brought up. Our grandmother—we call her GiGi—raised us after the plane crash that killed our grandfather and all of our parents. Ten kids is a lot to handle. But for it not to be constant war, we were taught a lot about cooperating with each other, about solving the problems and disagreements we had. I guess we learned really well how to get along and that crossed over into business."

"And was Howard or Mitchum your father?"

That could have been a loaded question given the history between his father and Howard, so Lindie was glad to say "Mitchum was my dad. There are six of us. I'm a triplet and we're the youngest. Along with our cousin Jani, who's our same age."

"You're a *triplet*?"

"With my sister Livi and our brother Lang."

"So Howard had—"

"Four kids. My cousins," she said a bit defensively in case he was going to say anything against them or their father. Then to redirect the conversation, she took a different tack. "Even though there are so many of us, though, we're easy to work with. Don't worry that it would be complicated to take us on as a client."

"Not going to happen," he reminded her, though he seemed amused.

"I'm just saying that you're welcome to talk to any vendor, any outsourcing, anyone we deal with, because you won't hear complaints that they don't know who they're answering to or are ever pulled in different directions by us. We're one solid unit, decisions are majority rule, and we all know how to cope with being on the losing side of a vote."

"Not a concern I have because you won't ever be my client." Again, he said that nicely but firmly.

But Lindie was persistent. She had to be to justify sitting there with him when her instincts were telling her to run while she still could.

"If you don't have plans," she said, "Camden Inc. could buy you dinner and we could talk about it." Just for business. Only for business. Not because she *wanted* to have dinner with him.

He shook his head as if she were incorrigible.

"Two things," he said. "I do have plans. Since I'm already in Wheatley on Thursdays, I take my son to dinner. And Camden Inc. will *never* buy me anything. That would look to my clients like a bribe."

Hmm. If having dinner with him really would have been for no reason other than business, why did she feel personally shot down?

It was stupid, she told herself.

Nevertheless that was how she felt. And rejection wasn't something she was accustomed to personally or professionally so she wasn't exactly sure how to respond.

Just then the last of the kids went out the front doors so Sawyer's job was done. He pulled his arms from the back of the bench and said, "That's it for us. We can take off."

There wasn't any *us* or *we*, she was tempted to point out in a miff, as if that would get back at him for the rejection of her dinner invitation. But she saw her petty response for what it was, reprimanded herself for it and merely stood when he did.

He held the center's front door open for her to go out ahead of him and they walked together to the parking lot.

"Where's your car?" he asked.

Lindie pointed to it and that was where he headed.

She wondered if his big white SUV was parked in the same general vicinity but after scanning the lot she spotted it at the opposite end.

So he was walking her to her car. That helped soothe the sting of her earlier thoughts that he'd arranged to have her assigned away from him and his so recent rejection, too.

"Are you still on board for tomorrow?" he asked along the way.

"I've already let them know at work that I'm taking the afternoon off," she informed him. "Shall I be here to help serve lunch to the kids or are you coming at one just to work on the park?" she asked, recalling what he'd told her of the Friday schedule.

"You're only coming for me?" he asked with a combination of challenge and something that sounded like satisfaction at the thought.

"Just asking," she said a bit aloofly because she wasn't willing to give his ego too much of a boost.

They'd reached her car. She unlocked and opened her door, standing on the inner side of it to look at him over the top of the window frame.

He finally answered her question. "I can't make it for the lunch. Huffman Consulting is sponsoring it. I'm having all the food sent in and served so the center staff and volunteers can have a treat in advance of the work, but I can't be here until one."

"So they won't need servers," Lindie concluded.

"No, but you're welcome to come and eat."

"I guess I'll see when I can get away and decide tomorrow," she said.

"And for tonight you can think of me eating dried-out macaroni and cheese to the mechanical serenade of robot bears," he said.

"But at least it won't be a *bribe*," she goaded.

He grinned and just stood there looking at her for a minute before he said, "We could have dinner another time maybe. As long as *I* pay."

Was he asking her out? Or just feeling guilty for turning her down? Had the impact of being rejected showed?

Oh, she hoped not.

Because she didn't like the thought of a pity invitation—or even the vague suggestion of one—she said, "And as long as I get to talk about you taking us on as a client."

He just laughed. She wasn't sure what that meant, but it called her glance to the creases that appeared at the corners of his eyes, to the lines that went from the sides of his nose to the corners of his mouth, to that mouth...

It was a good mouth. Sexy. And suddenly Lindie was thinking about it in terms of kissing.

Of him kissing her.

Of her kissing him back.

She was wondering what it would be like.

And guessing that it might be something he was particularly talented at because how could he be anything else with a mouth like that?

Then she caught herself and looked at a car that had just pulled into the lot as if she was all cool and calm and *not* suddenly wanting to know how the man kissed!

"I should let you get to dinner with your son," she said, reminding herself that he *had* a son and what her own stance on that was.

"Yeah, robotic bears wait for no man," he agreed, clasping the top of her car door and pulling it open a fraction of an inch more so he was in control of it as she got behind the wheel.

"Come tomorrow in clothes that can be washed," he warned then.

"Right. Because you're going to have me doing something *down and dirty*," she repeated what he'd threatened when they'd first talked about this, her tone holding the innuendo this time.

It made him grin but he didn't confirm or deny anything. He merely said, "See you tomorrow," before he closed her door and walked away.

Leaving her with the sight of a terrific rear end.

A terrific rear end that was not going to make it any easier to get the image of him out of her head.

Where it seemed to have taken up residence since she'd met him.

No matter how hard she tried to evict it.

Chapter Four

"Ooh! What is that?"

Even though she'd been the one to ask the question, Lindie wasn't at all sure that she wanted to know the answer. Along with Sawyer and two twelve-year-old boys, she had been cleaning storm drains since the Wheatley park cleanup project began on Friday afternoon.

She suspected that Sawyer had chosen that particular chore *because* it was the worst one that needed to be done and he was amused by the idea of a Camden doing it under his supervision.

But she doubted that there was much satisfaction in it for him. Because while she did follow him to the gutter, the two twelve-year-old boys—Tyler and Eric— insisted that she not be allowed to do more than wield the rake to drag the wet leaves and debris and muck out for Sawyer and the two of them to actually put in trash bags. As a result—and considering that they were all wearing thick gardening gloves—she wasn't even getting her hands dirty.

Unfortunately she also wasn't getting to talk to Sawyer because the boys were very intent on showing off and posturing and making sure Lindie found out about their sports achievements and accomplishments while they all worked.

"It's a dead rat," Tyler informed her, picking it up by its long tail to show her what she'd just pulled out of the drain.

At Lindie's recoil Eric said, "Don't make her look at it!"

"It's okay," Lindie said. "But I think it's more important that you don't touch it."

"Yeah, get rid of that," Sawyer advised.

Tyler deposited it in the trash bag.

"Maybe you shouldn't even rake," Eric suggested to Lindie. "It's gross."

Lindie caught Sawyer rolling his eyes, sighing and shaking his head. Before he could comment, Lindie said, "It's fine. Let's just get it done."

She wasn't quite sure what was inspiring the boys' chivalry today. She'd come prepared to get "down and dirty" and had worn a little white tank top underneath a pair of shapeless denim overalls she hadn't had on since doing yard work for her grandmother the summer between her sophomore and junior year of college.

Completing the nothing-but-functional outfit was a pair of ordinary canvas sneakers. After leaving work to change at lunch she'd brushed all of her hair into a plain ponytail.

But still the boys seemed intent on impressing her. Tyler took this opportunity to boast that he'd developed his rodent disposal skills because most of the time he was the man of the house now that his dad had had to return to over-the-road truck driving. Something that had happened when his oil-changing franchise had gone under because the Camden Superstore offered the same service.

Tyler referred to Camden Superstore scornfully and Lindie caught Sawyer's pointed gaze at her. She thought she could read his mind—these boys probably wouldn't think quite as highly of her if they knew her last name.

But he didn't give her away and she merely praised Tyler for being so helpful around the house while silently accepting the blame for yet another infraction.

It took until midafternoon to clear the drains and then the foursome moved on to breaking down old, decaying picnic tables that were to be replaced.

It was a less dirty job and Lindie was amused at how impressed Eric was at her skills with a screwdriver bit in a cordless power drill—talents gained helping to build Habitat for Humanity houses. It was something that Tyler called him on as if she needed defending.

"Girls can do things like that," Tyler said as if Eric had insulted her.

"But she's *such* a girl," Sawyer put in with some orneriness. "I think that's what makes it so surprising."

"I've never had complaints about that before," she countered.

"*I'm* not complaining about you being a girl!" Tyler pointed out.

"Me neither," Eric declared.

Sawyer sighed, adding under his breath, "Yeah, I'm not complaining, either."

And Lindie was left wondering why he'd said it at all if it was so reluctant.

The turnout had been good and headway was made on the park until dusk before an end was called. But there was still plenty left to be done and everyone was encouraged to come back on Saturday—and to return their gardening gloves and other tools to the community center before they left.

Volunteers, center employees and kids alike filed inside again to put away their supplies before people began saying good-night and heading out. Since Sawyer was helping to collect equipment, Lindie was, too, as both Tyler and Eric hung back for no good reason, still finding things to talk to Lindie about.

Until Sawyer said, "Okay, boys. Good work today. Thanks for all you did."

"Are you coming back tomorrow?" Eric asked Lindie.

Lindie looked to Sawyer for a clue as to whether or not he was. But he didn't give her one. Instead the arch of one of his eyebrows seemed to ask the same thing without imparting the information she wanted.

Counting on the likelihood that he was—and by then fully invested in helping these people anyway—she said, "I am."

She wasn't quite sure what Sawyer's small smile meant at that answer but it bore some resemblance to the smiles it elicited from the boys before Tyler said, "Then we'll be here, too."

Lindie heard Sawyer's sigh but she didn't think the boys did. Then he said, "Are you guys walking home or getting a ride?"

"Tyler's sleeping over and I just live across the street," Eric said.

"So we're walking," Tyler finished.

"Go on, then, before it gets completely dark," Sawyer commanded, putting an end to their lingering.

"We could wait and walk you out, too," Eric suggested to Lindie.

"Oh, for crying out loud," Sawyer muttered under his breath.

Lindie jumped in to say, "Thanks, but you guys go on. You must be starving. Go home and have dinner."

They stumbled over themselves saying goodbye to her but finally left.

"Apparently you've made two conquests," Sawyer said when they were gone.

Lindie wondered why he sounded so annoyed. "They did a lot of work, whatever the reason was. Isn't that a good thing?"

"Yeah, but...sheesh!" he said, exasperated.

"You just can't handle the competition?" Lindie asked with a straight face.

She wasn't sure whether he was going to be outraged or amused but his laugh was spontaneous. "I thought it was you who wanted to be with me," he shot back.

Had he been viewing today as *being with* her, instead of just an opportunity to show her a thing or two?

Hmm.

She left that alone, though. "And you knew I was volunteering to have the chance to talk to you so you picked the worst job on the list just so you could stick it to me. Did it disappoint you that the boys stepped in to make it easier on me?"

He grinned. "You didn't just say 'stick it to me.'"

Maybe not the best turn of phrase she could have chosen but she wasn't going to let him turn the tables on her.

"I didn't say it the way you're taking it. At least the boys aren't lechers!"

"Oh, you are kidding yourself, lady."

"They're nice boys."

"They are," he agreed. "Nice, *normal* boys. Who did not rush to help Marie or Mrs. Watley or lovely little Grace."

Marie and Mrs. Watley were both large and substantially matronly older women. And the "lovely little Grace" was thin and fit, but seventy-nine.

"And if they *had* worked with them," Sawyer added, "you can bet there wouldn't have been all that clumsy flirting."

"It was sweet. And funny," she said. Then she held up her palms and looked down at her overalls. "And it's not like I came dolled up, as my grandmother would say."

"I don't think it makes any difference how you dress," he said after a glance in the same direction and a return to looking at her face. "It might help if you put a bag over your head, but other than that..." He left the rest unsaid. "But please, don't come in anything 'girlier' tomorrow or one of those boys might actually keel over. Plus chaperoning the two of them is all I can take—if you attract any more minions I might lose it."

So he would be there tomorrow.

Rather than comment on that, Lindie went back to her earlier goad. "Because of the competition."

He laughed again. "You think I don't have better game than a couple of twelve-year-olds?"

Lindie shrugged.

"I'm gonna take you down the street and buy you a sub sandwich with anything you want on it just to prove it."

It was her turn to laugh. "Wow. Yeah. You *do* have game. Was that supposed to be an invitation to dinner?"

"A full twelve inches—if you want it. Piled high with whatever you take on it."

"Do I have to call Eric and Tyler back to chaperone *you*?"

"All right, all right, all right," he conceded with another smile and no repentance whatsoever. "What do you say? A sandwich down the street? You didn't come for the lunch today, so I'll buy you a half-assed dinner for your hard work."

And then she could talk to him and make some of the strides in getting to know him that she'd hoped to make while working with him today.

That was all there was to it.

It didn't have anything to do with the fact that as flattering as it had been to have the boys fawning over her, she felt a little robbed because she hadn't been able to talk to Sawyer.

"Deal," she said. "But if that's the extent of your game, it's pretty sad."

Taking their separate cars, Lindie followed Sawyer to the brightly lit sandwich shop.

She would have liked to be able to change into other clothes and do something different with her hair and makeup. But she hadn't come prepared for anything other than outdoor maintenance so she looked the same as when she'd left the park. And so did Sawyer, in jeans and a gray hoodie that somehow didn't dim his handsomeness one iota.

"I was surprised that so many people came out to help—even more of them tonight when they got off work," she said as they sat in one of the unpadded booths and unwrapped their sandwiches. He'd ordered the largest sandwich on the menu and still his hands dwarfed it.

Lindie tried not to notice, taking a bite of her much smaller turkey sub.

"Nobody is happy about what's happened to that part of Wheatley," Sawyer replied.

She really didn't want him on his soapbox again. The problems a Camden Superstore caused were becoming more and more clear to her on their own every time she was in Wheatley. It was Sawyer himself who she'd been assigned—and wanted—to get to know. So to keep from going down that other path again she said, "I wasn't sure whether you were working on the park tomorrow or if you had other plans."

"But you guessed right. You figured I'd be there so you said you would be, too."

"I like helping out," she said quietly. "So what have you signed us up for? Should I wear a hazmat suit?"

"Hmm. That might keep the boys away," he mused. "We're picking weeds. There's an overgrown area that needs to be cleared out for the chess pavilion."

"There's going to be a chess pavilion? Will there be a lot of use for that?"

"Actually, I'm sponsoring it for my own sake. There's one on the Sixteenth Street Mall down in Denver and a whole lot more of them in California—my family's vacation spot every year when I was growing up—where my dad and I would go to play. It was something I really liked doing with him so I lobbied for one here. I figured as long as we were fixing up this park anyway—"

"There's a big interest in chess in Wheatley?"

"I'm working on it." The chuckle that went with that

was wry and said the answer to her question was no, there wasn't an overwhelming interest in chess. Not yet, anyway. "I've taught a lot of the kids at the center. But like I said, the outdoor tables are really for my own sake. I got the agreement for it because I'm footing the bill. It'll only be four tables but I was thinking that it was something I wanted to do with Sam one day."

Two tiny frown lines creased the spot between his eyebrows, as if there was something else going on when it came to that subject. Lindie recalled having that same sense the first day they'd met when he'd said his son lived in Wheatley "for now."

"Sam is your son," she said, hoping to inspire him to open up about whatever was going on.

"Right. Sam is my four-year-old. So far we're just working on learning the pieces but I'm having trouble getting past the knights being horses and him making them charge through and knock down all the other pieces. We'll get there, though. My dad did with me and I will with Sam."

The mention of his father eased the frown and turned the corners of his mouth up.

Interpreting that, she said, "You have a good relationship with your dad and you want to duplicate it with your son."

"My dad is great," he stated simply.

Since that seemed like as good a segue as any to air out some of the past, Lindie said, "Tell me about your dad. I don't know anything about him except that he was engaged to my aunt Tina a long time ago."

"Tina. The debutante who was more in Howard Camden's league than my middle-class dad's and the engagement that nearly cost him his construction business."

Lindie's aunt Tina had been one of the children of an airline magnate and, yes, the Larson family had been close behind the Camdens on the social ladder.

"But my dad," Sawyer went on, "was—and still is even at sixty-eight—a good-looking guy who the ladies have always loved."

Sitting across the table from Sawyer and seeing for herself how drop-dead gorgeous he was, Lindie had no problem believing that his father had been a lady-killer. She did find it difficult to believe that he could have been any more attractive than his son. But her mind was wandering and she tried to rein it in and listen to what he was saying.

"So until Howard Camden pulled his sh—shenanigans—it didn't matter even to a debutante that he was in a lower tax bracket."

"Uncle Howard's *shenanigans*..." she repeated. "I'd like to hear your side of what happened."

"Why? Because you want to make sure you don't admit to something you don't have to?"

"Because I'm not sure I know the worst of it and I'd like to have the whole picture." Her grandmother had thought the journals left some things out, so they couldn't be certain in these situations if they had all the facts.

"My side of what happened." He took a bite of his sandwich, clearly to give himself time to consider whether or not to answer.

Lindie merely waited, eating a potato chip.

After a moment he'd apparently made his decision because he said, "According to my dad, he met Tina Larson when he did some work on the Denver Country Club. *She* asked *him* out the first time and they hit it off. She was even the one to start talking about marrying him. That was what led to him proposing. But Howard Camden wanted her—my dad says that he'd seen it when they'd all been at the country club or at parties and things at the same time. He said the guy couldn't take his eyes off her. He even flirted with her right in front of my dad after they were engaged. But my dad's not an insecure guy, he wasn't threatened. Tina was his and he wasn't worried about it. Instead he felt pretty much on top of the world—a beautiful rich girl had pursued him and wanted to marry him. He had his own construction company and it was doing well. He'd won bids on four different major projects so he needed to hire more people and expand. Top of the world," Sawyer repeated.

Another bite of sandwich, another pause. More silence from Lindie as she merely waited and listened when he spoke again.

"Dad was busy, but not so busy that he had to neglect Tina. Until things started to go wrong."

"Things like what?" Lindie asked.

"Expensive mistakes started being made in orders for materials. Wrong addresses for deliveries, then there were delays and extra costs for reloading and getting the materials to the right places. Shoddy workmanship caused all kinds of problems—failed inspections, time and money to bring things up to code, some damage to the company's reputation. Fights broke out among the workers, which had never happened before. There were walkouts. There were scheduling mistakes that left clients mad and put Huffman Construction in breach of contracts. The IRS suddenly came out of the woodwork to do an audit of the books—"

Instigated by a Camden connection within the IRS—

that was one of the things she knew. But she didn't tell him that.

Sawyer took a breath, shook his head and said, "Within months of getting engaged to Tina my dad was overwhelmed with business problems. The company was in serious trouble. He was on the verge of losing everything. He had an obligation to his workers and his clients to get things back in hand. His focus had to be on that. He had no choice but to spend long hours dealing with one disaster after another."

"And he needed to postpone his wedding to Aunt Tina on top of having hardly any time to spend with her."

"You got it," he confirmed. "My dad says that Tina was patient and understanding at first. But he'd had to leave her in the lurch over and over again and after a while…" Sawyer shrugged. "There were parties and country club functions, weddings of friends—not to mention celebrating their own engagement—and a whole slew of other social obligations that she wanted and needed to go to. She got tired of going to everything alone."

"Enter my uncle," Lindie supplied.

"Right. Enter Howard Camden. He ran in the same circles Tina did. He was at the same parties and weddings and whatnot. And there he was…understanding and sympathetic."

"And also handsome and charming and fun. That's how I remember my uncle."

"Little by little Tina was spending more time with him than with my dad. All the while—my dad had no doubt—Howard Camden was making it clear to her how much he wanted there to be more between him and Tina."

"Until there was."

"What put it over the top was a rumor that surfaced

that it wasn't only business keeping my dad busy. That he was having an affair with a woman who worked for him. He wasn't. But when Tina confronted the woman—encouraged to do so by your uncle—she confirmed the rumor."

Lindie cringed.

"That was it for Tina," Sawyer said. "She broke off the engagement and there good old Howard Camden was, waiting to comfort her."

Sawyer had finished his sandwich and his chips and he sat back, angled slightly on his side of the booth to prop an elbow on the seatback. "My dad could never prove anything," he told her. "But he'd heard about the Camdens—that they'd do anything to get what they wanted. When someone my dad hadn't slept with claimed he had, he started to piece things together. The woman in the office had started around the same time as a handful of construction workers. That was also when all the problems had started. Problems that stopped once he fired the woman and when the workers—having accomplished their mission—all quit. It wasn't hard to figure out that they were Camden plants to sabotage him, keep him busy and away from Tina so she could become open season for your uncle."

Lindie again didn't say anything, letting only her silence confirm it.

"My dad went to Tina to tell her what he suspected but with no way to prove it—because tracks had been well covered—she just didn't buy it. She said she was in love with Howard, she was going to marry him, and that was it."

"Was your dad heartbroken?" Lindie asked compassionately.

"And mad as hell," Sawyer said with a humorless laugh.

"But he recovered?" she asked even though she knew he had. GiGi's research had told them as much.

"It took some time. The woman who claimed to have had an affair with him had also made a mess of the books and he ended up owing the government back taxes and penalties. His business reputation had suffered a hit so the business came close to going under but he managed to pull it out of the fire."

"And he did end up married," Lindie pointed out.

"To my mom. He's always said that she was his reward for surviving what the Camdens did to him and that the lucky part of the whole thing was that it kept him free to meet the love of his life."

"So he ended up happy," Lindie concluded, trying to concentrate on the positive side.

Sawyer didn't answer immediately. He studied her so keenly that his crystal-blue gaze began to make her uncomfortable. "Yeah, he did. My dad ended up happy with my mom, he had my brother and me, his business turned around and made him a good living until he sold it so he and my mom could retire to Arizona a couple of years ago. But that doesn't excuse what your family did."

"I know," Lindie said quietly. "If it helps at all, my uncle really was head-over-heels in love with my aunt. He didn't think he could live without her." That was why H.J. and Howard's father, Hank, and brother, Mitchum, had gotten in on the scheme and participated with their own ideas and connections and contacts.

"Still doesn't excuse it."

"I know. You're right," she agreed. "The ends don't

justify the means. None of us condone what went on and we really are sorry for it."

He stared at her for another long moment before he let out a bit of a huff and said, "Uh-huh. You're all really sorry now that the shoe is on the other foot and I'm in a position where I can make some of *your* business life miserable. Because I don't see you in Arizona, talking to my dad—who's really the injured party here. Instead it's me you want to make nice with."

"If there's something I can do make it up to your dad just tell me and I'll get it done. But since, as you said, everything ended up working out for him, we just couldn't figure out what he might need."

"My dad doesn't need anything from you. Or want anything from you. But he does get a kick out of seeing me *stick it* to you all like your uncle and whoever else helped stick it to him."

"He likes revenge better than he'd like to see your business profits double or triple?"

Sawyer laughed sardonically. "I don't know," he said. "I haven't—and won't—tell him that's a possibility because it isn't. For the nth time—I'm not taking Camden Incorporated on as a client."

"We'll see," Lindie said.

"Yes, we will."

They'd both finished eating some time before and it was getting late so Sawyer crumpled up the sandwich's paper wrapper, signaling that it was time to put an end to this.

Lindie followed suit, slightly alarmed to discover that she was no more eager to end her time with him now than she had been before they'd had dinner.

And maybe, despite the fact that he'd initiated the

cleanup, Sawyer wasn't, either, because once they got outside he leaned against her car door rather than offer her free access to open it.

"So you really are going to show up again tomorrow?" he asked.

"Really am. Maybe helping clear the spot for your chess tables so you can share the same experience with your little boy will put a drop in the bucket of making things up."

"It all happened a long time ago," he said, looking very intently at her. "It doesn't need to be made up for at this point. It might have been the catalyst for what I do now, but what I do now is important in its own right. That's why I'm going to keep doing it," he warned yet again.

Lindie only smiled a small, confident smile at him and said, "I'm going to find a way that works for everyone."

He shrugged and gave her the same kind of smile. "You can go ahead and keep trying," he said as if failure was inevitable. But there was something else in his tone, too. In the glint of his blue eyes. Something that had the air of invitation. As if he liked that she was trying. Maybe as if he liked seeing her, having her around. Maybe as if he liked her...

He pushed away from her car door and took a step to stand directly in front of her. His eyes never lost contact with hers. And that sexy little smile never faded.

"Now I have a confession," he said quietly.

Lindie tilted her chin up, encouraging him.

"You've had some schmutz on your face since this afternoon and I didn't tell you."

"You made me come here for dinner with a dirty face?"

He grinned. "It's kinda cute," he said, raising an index

finger to the apple of her left cheek to rub at whatever was there.

There hadn't been any physical contact before that moment and while it wasn't much, it still packed a wallop for Lindie. For no reason she could explain, it set off a tingling sensation that was like a giddy little dance of excitement all around that spot.

The sensation took her by surprise. She wondered if he'd somehow felt it, too, because that cocky grin he'd started out with turned more curious and his brows pulsed together in a split second of what looked like confusion.

He traced all four tips of his fingers along the side of her face and said, almost more to himself than to her, "You have the softest skin."

Before she knew it was coming, he leaned over and kissed her. A quick peck that was there and gone before she'd even closed her eyes or registered it or responded.

Then it was over, his hand was gone from her face and he had a shocked, but amused, expression on his.

"How'd that happen?" he asked as if he hadn't been responsible.

Lindie asked the same thing but only with the arch of her own eyebrows.

"Want to hit me?" he offered.

She shook her head, unable to speak because what she wanted to say was *kiss me again.* And there was no way she could let herself do that!

"Still on board for tomorrow?" he asked, clearly testing to see if that kiss had changed her plans.

"Yes," she confirmed.

He grinned as if that pleased him, turned around and opened her car door for her.

Lindie got behind the wheel and glanced up at him,

trying not to wish that he would lean in to take advantage of her upraised face to kiss her again, after all.

Which—wishing for it or not—he didn't do.

Instead he told her to drive safe and closed the door before he went around to his SUV.

So Lindie started her car and pulled out of her parking spot, putting every effort into acting as if that dumb little nothing of a peck on the lips hadn't stunned her and left that tingle of excitement raining all through her.

But it had.

No matter how she acted.

It had.

Chapter Five

"Really? You have to be kidding. To pick weeds? Dumb ass!" Sawyer said to himself on Saturday morning.

He'd just finished shaving and, without thinking about it, had reached for the cologne that he never used unless he was going on a date.

What he *was* thinking about was the same thing he'd been thinking about since he'd met her. Lindie Camden. And thinking about her while preparing to spend the day with her had caused that automatic reach for the cologne. As if picking weeds with her was a date.

"Dumb, dumb, dumb ass!" he repeated as he pulled his hand away from the bottle without grabbing it and using the expensive ocean-breeze scented stuff inside.

I'm as bad as Eric and Tyler.

Worse, he amended. He was worse than Eric and Tyler when it came to Lindie. Sure the boys had tried to linger after Friday's work was finished to get a little more time with her. But he'd put a stop to that and sent them home. So *he* could get a little more time with her. *Without* the boys interfering and taking up all her attention.

And then he'd topped the whole thing off by kissing her.

Oh, yeah, he was a dumb ass all right.

Definitely worse than two hormonal twelve-year-olds. Put together.

She's a *Camden*!

That's what he mentally shouted at himself. The same thing he'd mentally shouted at himself all week long every time he realized he'd lapsed into yet another daydream about her. Every time he'd found himself restlessly counting the hours, the minutes, until he would see her again. Every time the image of her sprang into his mind complete with that long, lustrous hair and those super-blue eyes and that face and that body and even the sound of her voice…

"She's a *Camden*," he told his reflection out loud as he closed the medicine cabinet door to keep himself away from that cologne.

He wouldn't touch a Camden with a ten-foot pole.

Except that last night he *had* touched her.

Because of that smudge on her face.

The smudge was information he'd kept to himself until the evening was coming to an end, but not to embarrass her the way he'd made it seem. The little smear of dirt on the high crest of her cheekbone had actually looked so cute that he hadn't wanted her to get rid of it right away. He'd liked that one small mar to her perfection.

He'd liked it so much that once he wasn't going to be

the one looking at it, he'd wanted it gone, as if to make sure no one else got to see her that way.

More dumb ass stuff.

But that was what he'd been thinking when he'd wiped that smudge away.

What he hadn't expected was that something as small, as simple, as touching one lousy finger to her face, would jolt him the way it had. Would leave him incapable of taking his hand away once it was there. Would compel him to bend over and kiss her!

What the hell had gotten into him?

A Camden! She's a Camden!

Something in him had been shouting that even as he'd been headed for that kiss, and as a result nearly the minute he'd made contact he'd pulled out of it.

But he'd still made the contact. And he wanted to shoot himself for it.

It didn't make any difference that she was one of the hottest women he'd ever seen. Or that so far she seemed to be one of the nicest. She was still a member of a family he didn't approve of on any level.

And even if she wasn't, he had other things that needed his full and complete concentration. Other things to worry about. To fight. He had Sam. And he had that move to Vermont that could be looming. And a potential custody battle.

Plus he hadn't figured out what the hell he did wrong with the women in his life that kept leading him to disasters in his relationships.

Even if Lindie wasn't a Camden, he shouldn't be cultivating anything with her.

He certainly needed not to be touching her or kissing her—however innocently or briefly.

"It's not going to happen again," he told his reflection in the most threatening tone he could muster, as if the guy in the mirror was someone else.

But he meant it.

He wasn't going to touch her. He sure as hell wasn't going to kiss her.

He was going to make sure she understood all the harm her family had done and then he was going to walk away, deal with his own problems and go on being Camden Incorporated's worst nightmare.

There was no question. That was how this thing with her had to go.

In the meantime he was also going to ignore how stinking excited he was when he walked out of the bathroom, out of his bedroom, out of his house, knowing that he was on his way to her again.

"I am so-oo sorry!" Lindie apologized for what was probably the tenth time. "Really, you don't have to stay here with me. This is all incredibly embarrassing."

It was after six on Saturday evening and Sawyer had been sitting with her in a hospital emergency room for more than four hours.

What had seemed to be a hay fever reaction to the weeds they were clearing at the community center's park—a reaction Lindie was just trying to endure with aplomb—had turned serious when they'd reached some mold-laden sedentary water.

Because streets had been rerouted to accommodate the Camden Superstore, emergency response times to the east side of Wheatley were longer and Sawyer had decided they couldn't risk waiting for an ambulance. He'd put her in his SUV and raced for the hospital himself.

She'd been struggling for breath by the time they'd arrived and the ER staff had rushed her in.

The initial treatment had gotten her out of immediate danger. But they'd wanted to give her oxygen for a while and to keep an eye on her to make sure she was stable. Since the place was busy, there were long gaps between visits from the doctor or the nurses. The whole thing had resulted in hours and hours of sitting. With Sawyer by her side. And her trying to convince him that he didn't have to be.

"I'm not going anywhere," he said, also for about the tenth time.

Ordinarily, Lindie would have called someone in her family and the entire group would have rallied. But her cousin Seth and his wife had a week-old baby boy that everyone except her brother Lang had gone to Northbridge, Montana, to see. Lang and his wife weren't going until Sunday because they were in Vail for a wedding today, making him also too far away to get there. When a nurse had asked if there was anyone she wanted contacted and she'd explained the situation—with Sawyer there to hear it, too—he'd settled in and refused to leave.

But she was still trying.

"Really, when they release me I can call a cab to get me back to my car and—"

"You can't drive—they've pumped you so full of antihistamines and antianxiety drugs that you keep dozing off in the middle of sentences and you weave when you walk. I'm staying until they release you, then driving you home. I already called the Wheatley police during your last nap and explained that your car would have to stay in the community center's parking lot overnight. Tomorrow I'll pick you up and take you back to get it. That's the way it's going to be, and that's all there is to it."

He was all the more attractive when he took charge—it was something Lindie had noticed through the work at the park. But she had mixed feelings about his stubborn refusal to leave her on her own at the hospital.

On the one hand, she was grateful to him for getting her there, for keeping her company and looking out for her during a frightening situation.

On the other hand, she hated having him see her this way. She was certainly not at her best—vulnerable, panicked, loopy, in a hospital gown with a tube stuck in her arm and an oxygen cannula up her nose. And most likely with the makeup she'd applied that morning worn away and her hair in who knew what kind of mess.

While there he was, incredible looking even in a T-shirt and a pair of well-worn jeans. Jeans that he most definitely wore well, and an army-green T-shirt with the short sleeves stretched taut over noteworthy biceps and molded to muscular shoulders, chest and a very flat middle.

In comparison she felt at a disadvantage.

A male nurse came into the room to announce that the doctor had finally decided she could be released. The nurse went over her instructions with both Lindie and Sawyer before she signed the papers. Then Sawyer took them to keep track of and left the room while Lindie's oxygen and intravenous tubes were removed so she could get dressed.

Without a mirror in the room she still had no idea how she looked once she'd dressed in her own jeans, tennis shoes and a V-necked yellow T-shirt.

She retrieved a brush from her purse and took her hair

out of the pigtails she'd put it in that morning. Then she ran the brush through it and let it hang loose, hoping the rubber bands hadn't left ugly ridges.

But that was the best she could do—and really all she was up to doing—before she left the tiny cubicle of a room.

Expecting to find Sawyer right outside, she was surprised that he wasn't. She paused, looking up and down the corridor, but she still didn't see him. Unsteady and disoriented, she wasn't sure which way was the way out.

The male nurse happened by, pointed and said, "He's right around the corner."

Lindie thanked the nurse and walked on slightly wobbly legs in the direction he had indicated.

It was an odd relief when she rounded the corner and there Sawyer was.

His back was to her and as she headed for him she couldn't help noticing yet again that the rear view was as good as the front, making her want to get closer to him the way she always did. But as she got nearer she realized that he was talking to four little girls she recognized— the Murphy sisters—and that there was a police officer nearby.

"Lindie!" the youngest of the Murphy girls said when she spotted her approaching them all. "My gramma got sick!"

Lindie could tell by the sober expressions that that didn't mean anything good as she joined the group.

"What happened?" she asked.

Sawyer answered. "Their grandmother had a stroke. They think they've stabilized her but they're moving her into intensive care."

And their grandmother was their guardian because Dad had passed away and Mom had gone to prison.

"She'll be okay, though," Lindie said softly to Sawyer, hoping for something that sounded like encouragement.

The arch of Sawyer's eyebrows didn't give it. "The doctors are taking good care of her."

"And the girls?" she said equally as softly.

"Officer Brown here has called in social services. Their caseworker is on her way. Do you think you're up to waiting with them?"

Lindie didn't hesitate. "Absolutely."

They were asked to move out into the lobby then. The police officer stepped up as if to enforce a command and Angel, the oldest of the Murphy girls, took Clara's hand. "Come on," she said, leading her sisters toward the exit from the treatment rooms with the police officer tagging along.

"We'll be right there," Lindie told them, hanging back to talk to Sawyer.

"How bad is it?" she asked when the girls were out of earshot.

"It isn't good. Gramma hasn't regained consciousness and she isn't responding to pain stimuli. I'm just repeating what I was told. I'm not sure what that means except that they said it wasn't a good sign."

"And she's all they have?"

"I'm not sure."

"Where will they go if she is?"

"Foster care."

Lindie shook her head emphatically. It wasn't in her nature to sit idly by when someone needed help. And while she was trying to curb some of those impulses because they'd gotten her into sticky situations—that had most recently even put her in danger—there was no way she could walk away from those four girls.

"They can come home with me," she said without hesitation. "I have a house and empty bedrooms and—"

"Hold on!" Sawyer cautioned. "You can't just do something like that."

"Yes, I can," she insisted, adrenaline pumping through her to make her feel more on top of things suddenly. "I don't want to see them just stuck somewhere or split up."

"I understand how you feel, but they may have other family to go to. Maybe family that isn't as close as Gramma but an aunt or an uncle or a cousin or somebody. This may be a long-term thing, Lindie, if Gramma doesn't make it or she's permanently disabled or even if she's in for a long recovery period before she can handle four little girls again."

"Still," Lindie said, undaunted.

"No, not *still*. You're half out of it and even if you weren't, there's no way I'd let you sign on right here and now, before you've thought it through, for what could turn out to be a substantial commitment to these girls. We're going to stay with them so they aren't alone with strangers until their caseworker gets here. Then we'll listen to what the caseworker has to say and—"

"I don't want them to go into foster care for even one night. If that's the only option, I'm taking them home with me."

"Okay, if foster care is where they'll need to go tonight, then *maybe* you can volunteer. But promise me you won't volunteer until we find out if that *is* where they need to go."

When she didn't immediately agree he said, "Promise

me or I *will* put you in a cab to get you out of here before you do something you shouldn't."

He made the threat firmly enough for her to believe that was exactly what he would do, so she took a breath and made the promise, conceding not to rush into anything and reminding herself that that *did* often get her into trouble.

Neither of them said anything else as they left the treatment area and went into the lobby where the girls were watching anxiously for them. Apparently the young cop saw his position as solely observational because he wasn't talking to them at all.

Sawyer insisted that Lindie sit in the remaining empty chair in the row of five with the girls and he stood in front of them all.

Once she was settled, the girls spontaneously launched into the story of finding their grandmother on the kitchen floor, of Angel dialing 9-1-1, of riding in a police car behind the ambulance that had brought their grandmother to the hospital.

The social worker arrived in the lobby about the time the story was finished and the girls greeted her by name. They seemed happy to see her, which helped ease some of Lindie's concerns.

The police officer also knew the caseworker and Sawyer introduced himself and Lindie, explaining that they knew the girls from the community center and had just happened to be at the hospital today, but wanted to make sure the sisters were taken care of before they left.

The social worker included them as she explained that she'd already spoken to an aunt on their father's side that was willing to have them stay with her.

"It might be a little crowded with your three cousins

but your aunt said you've had sleepovers there before and it will be like that. Only this will be for more than one night so I want you girls to be on your best behavior and help out where you can, okay?" the social worker said.

The girls didn't seem to have a problem with that idea and when Lindie glanced at Sawyer he raised an eyebrow at her as if to say, "See? There were other options."

After handing the Murphy girls over to their caseworker, Officer Brown returned to the treatment area, and Lindie and Sawyer walked out with them.

Lindie couldn't resist hugging the girls goodbye and telling them everything was going to be all right. She just hoped she wasn't lying to them and silently vowed that she'd do whatever she could to help them if other needs arose.

Then, before she knew it, she was once again in Sawyer's passenger seat and he was slipping in behind the wheel.

"I hope they'll be okay," she breathed as he pulled out of the parking lot and she glanced over her shoulder to see the girls getting into the social worker's car.

"We'll keep tabs on them and make sure they are," he said before asking for her home address and programing it into his SUV's guidance system.

He headed for the highway to get back to Denver and the next thing Lindie knew she was waking up to the sound of Sawyer's voice ordering hamburgers.

"Did I fall asleep again?" she asked, embarrassed.

He finished placing the order at the drive-through's menu board and pulled forward as instructed. "Out like a light," he confirmed.

"I'm sorry," she apologized for what seemed like bad

manners even though she knew the medications the hospital had given her were to blame.

"No big deal," he assured her with a small laugh.

"You're probably thinking it's a good thing I'm not trying to take care of four kids like this."

"Who me? Nah," he said facetiously as he picked up their food and drove on to her house only blocks away.

He didn't wait to be invited in and Lindie was still fumbling to unfasten her seat belt when he was already out and around to open her door for her. She did manage to find her keys in her purse as they went from her double-car driveway to the front door of her large, cottage-style ranch home.

"Nice place," he observed as she led him into the entry and closed the door behind them.

"Thanks. It needed a lot of remodeling but I've been here almost three years and I think the work is finally done." And she was finished decorating it in whites and warm blue hues in a country style that was more about comfort and big, fluffy-cushioned furniture than about formality or impressing anyone.

"Let's eat in the kitchen. Maybe I'll be able to perk up at the table." She led him to the rear of the house where she flipped on the lights to the space that had been the last of the remodel and now had a French-rustic feel to it.

"Brace for this," she warned. "Remember I told you I have four dogs? They'll come charging in any minute."

Her pets used a doggy door to go in and out to the backyard as they pleased. Since they hadn't been at the front to greet them Lindie knew they must be outside but would see the kitchen lights and come in.

That was exactly what happened and a moment later there were four dogs rallying around them.

"This is Harry and Max. They're labradoodles."

"Part Labrador, part poodles?"

"Right. And that's Walter. He's just a mutt. And the seven-pound alpha who keeps them all in line is Stan. You can tell he's part poodle and something else, but I don't know what."

"You weren't kidding about no purebred show dogs."

"They're all rescues. Harry and Max each needed hip replacements and their owners didn't want anything to do with that so they were going to have them put down. I'd met the vet at a benefit and he called me. The owners didn't want to keep them even if I paid for the hip replacements, so I took them—"

"And had hip replacements on *dogs*?"

"Yes, hip replacements on dogs," Lindie said before finishing her explanation. "Walter and Stan were both picked up as strays—they'd been on the streets and were nearly starving. Poor Stan only weighed three pounds. But as you can see by Walter's girth, he's made up for it, and even Stan has some meat on his bones now."

After petting all four dogs and watching Sawyer indulge them, as well, Lindie gave them bones so they would leave them alone.

"Okay, dog hellos are done," she said, turning to Sawyer. "What can I get you to drink? I have soda or juice or iced tea."

"A glass of water would be fine, thanks. But why don't you sit and I'll take care of that."

"I'm fine. Just dopey." She took out two glasses, filled them with ice and water from the dispenser in the freezer door and set them on the big antique oak table surrounded by metal café chairs.

"Since you were sleeping when I ordered I just got

cheeseburgers with the works. Take off whatever you don't want on yours," he advised as he divided what was in the bag and they both sat to eat.

"So. First the candy bars. Now this tonight with the Murphy girls. Do you always leap before you look?"

"It's a bad habit."

"At least a habit, anyway, because I guess you even did it with volunteering at the center. I thought that was just to get to me but now I'm not so sure," he mused. "But volunteering at the center and slipping contraband candy bars to kids is one thing. Taking on four kids in the blink of an eye for what could be months is something else."

"I told you that my grandmother took in me and my brothers and sister and cousins when we didn't have anywhere else to go. That was unsettling enough. But if I'd been separated from my brothers or my sister and shuffled off to people I'd never even met before?" She shook her head. "That would have been so much worse. I don't know the Murphy girls well, but I like them, and if they need my help they'll get it."

"Like the four dogs," he said with a glance at her pets. "Have you always brought home strays?"

"Every single one I've ever found. Cats, dogs and a duck once that still lives on the pond at my grandmother's house."

He'd just taken a bite of burger but as he chewed he studied her. "You're the Camden rescuer?"

"When there's not a need for an assassin," she said as if it were fact, making him laugh.

Then, sobering, he said, "So, I don't know details, but I have some general knowledge of the history of the Camdens—the plane crash, for instance. But how was it that so much of your family was on that plane in the first place? Everybody but H.J. and your grandmother and you kids."

"There was a vacation for the adults planned. My sister and brothers and I were supposed to be left with our nanny, and my cousins with theirs. But H.J. was living with my grandmother and grandfather by then and he hurt his back just before they were set to leave. GiGi stayed home to take care of him or they would have been lost, too."

"How old were you?"

"Lang, Livi and I—and our cousin Jani—were the youngest of the kids. We were six."

"And your grandmother took in all ten of you?"

"She did."

"That's a whole lot of kids."

"A *whole* lot!" she confirmed. "It was a houseful. No doubt about that."

"A big Cherry Creek mansionful."

"Still a houseful. And we were lucky to have each other. It isn't always easy being who we are."

"It wasn't always easy being spoiled and pampered?" he goaded with enough humor in his voice to temper it.

"Ha! You don't know my grandmother! We were *not* spoiled and we were definitely not pampered. GiGi was a farm girl from Montana, and money or no money, she made sure we were raised as much the way she had been as possible. Nannies were out of the question. We had chores. Even the smallest of us and even when we were little, bitty kids. When we got older we all had to get jobs if we couldn't make our allowances stretch far enough for the things we wanted—which none of us could so we all had the usual teenage part-time jobs. We also had strict rules we had to follow, and GiGi never let us forget that with the Camden name came responsibilities and an obligation to give back, to do for others, to help wherever we could."

"Like bringing home dogs and cats and ducks, and this stuff I'm seeing now."

"I guess I took what I was taught seriously." Lindie finished her hamburger and picked at her fries. "I know sometimes I go overboard. I just want to make sure everything and everybody is taken care of and has what they need, what they want. It's what I do. I'm uncomfortable thinking that anyone might be unhappy or not feel safe."

"Because you didn't?"

"I did."

"Not at first. How could you have?" he said as if he'd seen through her. "At first you were just a six-year-old who lost both of your parents. No matter what your last name was, that would shatter any kid's world. And then, as if it wasn't enough to be one of six at home, you had to move and become one of *ten*."

His insight was spot-on.

"I did have to compete for adult attention and my place in the sun," she admitted. "Actually, I can remember worrying about my place in the family and thinking that I had to be good, that I had to help wherever I could and make myself useful and not rock the boat or GiGi might wash her hands of me to make things easier."

"Wow! That had to be a scary thought for a tiny kid! And somehow that turned into you wanting to become the help and salvation and safe haven for whoever might feel the same way?"

Lindie laughed. "I never considered that, but maybe that's true. Only now it's kind of gotten out of hand and my family wants me to tone it down. Which I'm honestly trying to do," she said. "I'm trying not to always swoop in to rescue everyone. In the past few years it's made trouble for me with friends and with men in my life. Three months ago it got me hurt and put me in danger, so my whole family wants me to put some brakes on it now."

"Hurt and in danger?"

"I can't say no. I can't pass a donation jar without putting something in it. I can't not give to a charity or buy the stuff kids sell to support their schools or teams or scout troops. I haven't ever *not* signed on for anything that seemed like a worthy cause. And when it comes to panhandlers on the street or in parking lots—"

"You open your wallet," he interrupted with a note of ominousness.

"Three months ago I did that and it turned into a mugging. The guy grabbed my wallet and then wanted my purse, too. In the process of yanking it off my shoulder he knocked me down. I hit my head and got all bruised and scraped up."

"That's bad."

"Luckily another man came around the corner about that time. The panhandler ran off and my good Samaritan called for help. I ended up in the emergency room that day, too."

"How hurt were you?"

"A minor concussion, cuts and bumps and bruises. Nothing big."

"Big enough," he said as if convinced she was understating, his handsome face pulled into a frown.

"Well, yeah, big enough and sort of the frosting on the cake of some other things that my urge to fix and rescue have caused in my personal life. Anyway, what started as a kid has gone a little too far. My family has been telling me for a long time that I can't save the world and I'm starting to think they're right so I'm trying to control it some."

"By almost taking four kids home with you tonight?"

Lindie shrugged.

"What would have happened if you had?" he asked, watching her closely. "If you had done that and then regretted it, would you have just kept them and resented it? Resented them?"

That seemed like an odd question. "Is that why you didn't want me to do it? You thought I'd sign on for it and then regret it and resent them?"

He took a turn at shrugging.

"When I commit, I commit," she declared. "Don't you?"

"Yeah, *I* do. But..." He shook his head and seemed to concede to something. "Okay, maybe that came out of my own stuff. Maybe you *would* have been fine instantly becoming the mother of four for an indefinite amount of time or maybe even forever. But I guess the same way you're trying to control some excessive urges to fix and rescue, I'm trying to make sure that people don't agree to things they don't really want to agree to."

"That's something you've run into a lot?"

"Enough." He didn't expand, though. Instead he went on to lecture her again. "Like I said over the candy bars, when it comes to the kids at the center, watch and listen and ask questions, but *don't* leap before you look. Or before you talk to experts and explore options and make sure you aren't doing yourself or them a *dis*service. When it comes to your trying-not-to-fix-and-rescue thing, try a little harder, would you? Taking on four kids is not the same as taking on four dogs—although four dogs is a *lot* of commitment, too."

That seemed to conclude his lecture because he stood and began to gather the remnants of their dinner to stuff back in the bag. "I should take off and let you recuperate from today."

Lindie really was worn out so she had to agree, even though she wished he didn't have to go.

"I'm sorry that I kept you from clearing the spot for your chess tables," she said as she stood, too, and took the bag from him to take to the trash.

"The work went on, anyway. Marie called to see how you were and said that Eric and Tyler kept at it," Sawyer said as they headed for the front door.

"It was nice of Marie to call. And, see, Eric and Tyler weren't just trying to impress me."

"Right…" he said, making the word multiple syllables of sarcasm as they reached the entry, stopped and he turned to face her.

"One look at me at the hospital or now would change their minds for sure," she said, still feeling self-conscious about having Sawyer see her this way.

"Are you kidding? Those guys would have killed for a peek in the back of that hospital gown."

"I tried to make sure it was always closed!" she said, alarmed that *he* might have gotten a peek.

He laughed and she couldn't help admiring how great he looked when amusement drew lines on his face.

Oh, who was she kidding? She couldn't help admiring how handsome he was no matter what.

"Relax. I didn't see anything," he assured her. Then, looking closely at her, he smiled a small smile and added,

"Or anything earlier or now that would stop those boys from crushing on you."

He'd had the same glint in his eyes the night before just before he'd kissed her. Was he going to kiss her again now?

Her pulse picked up some speed at that thought but when nothing happened she hurried to say something to fill the gap.

"I know there's more work on the park scheduled for tomorrow but I can't be there," she said apologetically. "Lang and his wife are joining everybody in Northbridge for the day to see the baby but Lang's little boy— Carter—is just getting over a cold and they don't want to bring him around a newborn. So I'll have him for the day." Then she thought of something else and said, "Oh, I'll have Carter but no car—that's still in Wheatley."

"How old is Carter?"

"Three and a half."

"Actually, I'm not working at the center tomorrow, either," he told her. "Sam's mom is dropping him off at my place for the day." He hesitated. Then, sounding tentative, he said, "Since the boys are almost the same age, we could let them have a playdate and I can drive wherever we go. When I take Sam back to Wheatley tomorrow night I could drop you off to pick up your car."

A playdate for the boys, not a date-date for the grown-ups.

But still she'd get to see him.

And that pleased her in a way that had nothing to do with why she was *supposed* to be spending time with him.

How could she help that, though, when he was so easy on the eyes? When he was nicer than she had expected him to be? When he was kinder, more understanding and considerate and grounded and caring and intelligent? Not to mention that he was good-natured and funny and so, so much sexier than she wished he was?

None of that was part of her assignment and she shouldn't be fostering any kind of attraction to him. But there he stood. Looking the way he looked. And giving her the chance to spend tomorrow with him.

It just wasn't in her to say no.

"That would help me out. I'm always afraid I'm not exciting enough for Carter on my own and without a car... He'd play with the dogs for a while but if we just had to hang around here he'd hate it."

"Think he can play with the dogs until noon? Candy is bringing Sam at eleven-thirty."

"That should be about how long the dogs and I can entertain him."

"Noon then," he confirmed. "I promised Sam I'd take him to the Adventure Kingdom."

"I don't know what that is."

He grinned. "Well, tomorrow you'll get to learn. If it was winter we'd go to one of the indoor places but since we still have some warm weather to cash in on, this one is outside. There are trampolines, tree houses, bouncy houses, a maze, an inflated castle, a whole pirate ship. Kids love it."

"Oh, Carter would, that's for sure!" she said, knowing that this would be one visit with Aunt Lindie that wouldn't disappoint him.

"So we're on," Sawyer concluded. "Go see if you can sleep off the rest of those drugs and we'll hope we don't get anywhere near any moldy water tomorrow."

"Or instead of trampolines and tree houses and castles

and pirate ships there'll be gurneys and wheelchairs and so many other entertainments," she said.

He laughed, something she loved making him do.

"Yeah, every bit as much fun but let's try for Adventure Kingdom instead, huh?"

"Sure, if you want to settle for less."

He was still very focused on her, still smiling, but he wasn't showing signs of leaving.

He took a breath and said, "Yeah. I'm going."

"Thanks for everything you did today," Lindie said belatedly, so lost in looking into those crystal-blue eyes that she'd almost forgotten her manners.

"I really just hung around."

"I appreciate it, though. Nobody *wants* to hang around a hospital emergency room."

"I was glad to do it," he said as if he meant it.

All at once he clasped her shoulders in two big hands and leaned in.

And Lindie just knew he was going to kiss her this time and her heart raced once more and she tilted her chin and she was ready.

Only the kiss he gave her was on the forehead.

The forehead.

Deflating her every hope instantly.

Then his hands were gone and he was at the door, opening it and going outside.

Lindie forced herself to act as if having him kiss her on the forehead happened every day.

"Drive safe," she said.

"Sleep well," he countered.

And off he went.

Lindie closed the door, slumped against it and frowned at the four dogs who were all sitting in a row watching.

"I guess we're going backward," she told them. "Last night he at least hit the lips—even if it was for only a fraction of a second. Tonight all I got was hands on the shoulders, kiss on the forehead. Probably the way he says good-night to his son."

But what was she saying? And thinking and feeling?

She and Sawyer Huffman shouldn't be going anywhere when it came to kissing.

They shouldn't be kissing!

But still…

Should or shouldn't, she couldn't help *wanting* him to kiss her.

For real. On the mouth. Long enough to feel it. To experience it. To kiss him back.

"Uh-uh, I can't," she said to her dogs as if they'd encouraged her. "I can't get into anything with this man."

And she wouldn't.

She really, really wouldn't. Not when he was completely opposed to everything Camden. Not when he was their adversary. If anything could rattle her place in the family loose it could be that.

She just had to figure out how to stop the attraction to him and still do what she needed to do with him.

Then it occurred to her that tomorrow she would meet his son. She would see him with the child, which was that one thing she absolutely didn't want to come along with a relationship.

That would make it real for her. That would cement for her the fact that he was all wrong for her.

Surely after that she wouldn't have any more problems with this stupid attraction to him.

"That will do it," she assured her dogs as if they'd been privy to her thoughts.

That was the reason she couldn't wait for tomorrow to come, she told herself.

Just so she could meet Sawyer's son and put an end to whatever it was that seemed to be developing on the personal side of things.

And that should have been the *only* reason she couldn't wait for tomorrow to come.

Except that it wasn't…

Chapter Six

"Hey, Sean, what's up?" Sawyer greeted his brother as he answered the phone on Sunday morning.

"Just checking in to see what you're up to," his older brother answered.

"I have Sam today. I'm waiting for Candy to drop him off. You aren't calling to tell me something bad, are you? We didn't get that written-notice-to-relocate thing you said we could get from her, did we?"

As his business attorney and brother, Sean was informally overseeing his family law lawyer and tended to be the one to relay news. Sean had been the one to explain the process they would have to go through if Candy and her husband made the decision to move. He'd told Sawyer that a written notice to relocate would be the first official step. Sawyer knew if that happened the whole thing would move from tense talks to a court battle so he was on edge about it.

"That would come during the work week and do you really think I wouldn't call you the minute it came in? So far we're not in the woods with that yet. Have you heard something? Is it coming?"

"I haven't heard anything new, no. But I told you, the last time I talked to Candy she put me off, told me I should talk to her husband. I know that means she's avoiding the confrontation. There wouldn't be a confrontation if all she had to say was that they weren't going to move."

"The courts can't stop either of you from relocating. I told you that. The issue will be what the court decides is best for Sam and who gets custody of him in what state, not whether or not Candy and her husband would be allowed to move."

"I know," Sawyer admitted with disgust at the predicament he was in. "And the court is more likely to decide Sam should be with her. Even if it's in Vermont and I'm in Colorado."

"It'd help if you were married. At least that would give us the argument that, when you have to travel for work, Sam's everyday life wouldn't be disrupted because his stepmother would be there as usual. That would give you better ground to fight from. Is there anybody you could whisk away to Vegas for a quickie wedding?"

"No." Why did the image of Lindie come to mind when his brother asked that question? That made no sense at all.

"Are you even dating anybody?" Sean asked.

Lindie popped into his head again. But they weren't dating.

Although he wasn't sure how spending yesterday together qualified. He could have left her in the hospital rather than sit with her that whole time. And today? He could have *not* set up what he'd set up for today and avoided seeing her altogether. But he was leaving town for all of next week and something he didn't quite understand had made him want to see her the day before he left.

But to say they were dating? That wasn't true.

"No, I'm not dating anyone," he said firmly to his brother, reminding himself that even if he was interested in dating someone it wouldn't be Lindie. It wouldn't be a Camden. And it wouldn't be someone as headstrong as she'd proved to be over those candy bars and over the Murphy girls yesterday.

When he was ready to date again he wanted a reasonable, agreeable, easygoing woman who was open—really, really open—and honest about her feelings and what she did and didn't want. And not someone who just acted as if she was reasonable, agreeable and easygoing and then expected him to figure out when things weren't truly going as well as they seemed to be—that was what kept getting him into trouble.

But headstrong, stubborn and determined, which was what Lindie was, didn't translate as reasonable, agreeable or easygoing to him. So, no, they weren't dating and even if he was looking to date someone, it wouldn't be her.

"You're a good dad," his brother was saying into his thoughts about Lindie, dragging him back into the conversation. "Maybe Candy will think about how wrong it would be to take Sam away from that and convince old Harmon not to do it."

"Yeah, maybe," Sawyer said glumly. "But I think we'd better hope he comes to it himself because Candy isn't likely to do anything to influence the situation in my favor."

"Well, even if it happens, we'll do everything we can to get Sam back here as much as possible. Whole summers, every week he has off from school, holidays. We'll pull out all the stops to get you the fun times, and she and Harmon can do the dirty work."

Sawyer knew his brother had good intentions so he didn't tell him that he didn't want to even miss out on the less fun parts of his son's life.

"How about that Camden woman?" Sean asked.

"I'm not marrying her!"

"Huh?" his brother said, confused. "I was just asking if she was still hanging around trying to get you to take Camden Incorporated on as a client or if she'd given up yet."

Of course. He'd told Sean about Lindie and what she wanted. What else would his brother be asking about?

"Yeah, she's still hanging around, giving it the old college try," he said, hoping to cover his tracks.

It didn't work.

"Are you getting into something with her?" Sean asked suspiciously.

"No, no, no. It's just that…you know…she's the only female in my age bracket I see outside of work these days and you were talking about somebody for a quickie wedding."

"And you thought I was suggesting a *Camden*?"

"I just missed that you were changing the subject."

"She's hot, isn't she?"

"Smokin'—so what?"

"Man, you wouldn't, would you?"

"Wouldn't what? Marry her? Date her? Do anything with her? No, no and no again." Although there had been that damn drive to kiss her. Again. For the second night in a row.

At least last night he'd kept it to a pretty platonic one on the forehead.

But, wow, had it been tough to keep it at that! How was it possible for something as bland as the feel of her shoulders in the palms of his hands to be meaningful enough for him to keep reliving it?

Sean didn't say anything and the silence spoke volumes about how little his brother believed him. But Sean didn't argue. Instead he pretended to buy it. "Yeah, sure. You and a Camden? No way."

This was not going well and Sawyer decided he'd better get out before it got any worse. "I think Candy and *Harm* just pulled up so I'd better go. I'll be in Idaho all of next week but I'll call you from there to check in. And if we get anything from Candy's lawyer—"

"I'll be on the phone to you after I've read the first line."

"Thanks," Sawyer said before they exchanged goodbyes and hung up.

At which point Sawyer gave himself a stern talking-to about Lindie Camden and what the hell he was doing with her.

But it didn't change much.

When he was finished he was still counting how many more minutes had to pass until he could get to her today.

And wishing he wasn't going to be away from her for the next full week.

Adventure Kingdom was a big hit and for the first time Lindie didn't feel as if she'd disappointed or bored her nephew. Carter seemed to have one of the best times she'd ever seen him have.

He connected with Sam—who was the image of Sawyer and had the same blue eyes—and since Sam knew his way around the play park and was slightly older, Sam took the lead with her shorter, darker-haired nephew who bore the stamp of a Camden.

But as much as Carter seemed to like Sam, Lindie thought he liked Sawyer even more. And watching what went on with the two boys vying for Sawyer's attention became an example to Lindie of why she was right to avoid getting involved with a man who already had a child.

During her growing-up years she'd learned a whole lot about how it felt to be on the waiting list for attention, about agonizing about being overlooked. Or worse, that her grandmother might like one of her siblings or her cousins more.

GiGi had never showed any favoritism. She'd always been thoroughly fair and caring and treated them all equally, so there was no real basis for Lindie's insecurities. Yet Lindie had feared that if she didn't shine she might really get lost in the crowd. Or worse yet, lost altogether from a family so large.

She'd felt a sort of desperation to be reassured that she was as important as everyone else. She'd had a constant fear and worry that she might not make the grade in comparison, that she might somehow fall short, that everyone else might have more to offer.

And she'd met friends with half siblings who'd shared those worries.

As an adult she realized what she'd told Sawyer the night before—that those feelings had been a silly insecurity, that they were unfounded. But they were still emotions that she didn't want her own children to ever experience. Feelings that hadn't always been unfounded for friends with half siblings who *had* showed them up, that parents *had* seemed to favor.

And Sunday, as she watched what went on with Sam and Carter, it seemed to bring home to her that she needed to hold out for a man who didn't already have a child or children.

Sawyer was as good with Carter as he was with his own son. There was no faulting that. He made sure to give Carter a turn at everything he did with Sam.

But she saw with her own eyes that the boys worked harder and harder for Sawyer's approval. That they competed more and more for his praise and encouragement. That they showed off for him and tried to outdo each other. That a subtle rivalry developed. Then there were also the times when Sam pointed out emphatically that Sawyer was *his* dad, not Carter's.

This was only one day for both boys, Lindie told herself. It wasn't something either of them would deal with ever again or anything that was likely to impact them on any real or long-lasting level.

But that didn't make it any easier for her to witness moments of disappointment and resentment when poor little Sam was left cooling his heels and obviously jealous of the attention being taken away from him. As she saw moments of dejection and what looked like rejection in her nephew when he was on the sidelines while Sawyer's attention went to Sam.

Of course Lindie did all she could to entertain whichever boy wasn't being roughhoused by Sawyer when it happened, but he was the hero of the day and the one they were striving to impress no matter what she did. It brought home to her why she'd decided long ago that she wouldn't get involved with a man who already had kids.

It was too bad, though, she found herself also thinking.

Because Sawyer was a great dad. Attentive, caring, firm when he needed to be, indulgent but not overly permissive, protective without stifling, playfully one-of-the-guys when he could be. Exactly the kind of father she wanted for her own kids one day.

But for her kids alone.

Not for her kids and the kid he had before hers.

And, somehow, even as she told herself this was a good thing to see, a good reminder for her, it also made her a little sad.

They stayed at Adventure Kingdom until it closed. Lindie agreed to dinner at an arcade where there were activities and games for kids Sam and Carter's age. It was nearly eight o'clock when they finished and both boys were so worn out that they fell asleep on the way to Sam's house.

Lindie waited in the car with Carter while Sawyer lifted his son out of his car seat and carried him up to a house more upscale than what she'd seen nearer to the community center.

At first as she watched Sawyer approach the house she merely enjoyed the sight she'd been enjoying all day of him in jeans and a green polo shirt. The man could certainly do justice to a pair of jeans, and carrying the weight of his four-year-old made his biceps bulge alluringly.

When he reached the house he had to do some comical maneuvering to ring the door bell with his elbow and that made her laugh.

Her amusement was short-lived, though, when the front door opened. Two people answered the bell. The tall, attractive blond woman who Lindie assumed was Sam's mother took the boy out of Sawyer's arms and disappeared back into the house. To Lindie's surprise, the man remained to talk to Sawyer.

Lindie thought he was likely the stepfather Sam had mentioned during the day. He was tall but not quite as tall as Sawyer, stockier and clearly not as fit or as handsome, either, Lindie noted.

She couldn't hear what the two men were discussing but their expressions were serious and tense. And after a few moments their voices grew louder. Still not loud enough for Lindie to hear anything through the closed windows that kept the air-conditioning contained inside the car, but loud enough for her to know that neither man was happy with the other.

Finally, Sawyer returned to the car and got behind the wheel again, saying nothing, a deep frown beetling his brows.

Whatever had gone on on that doorstep was none of her business and since Sawyer didn't offer any information— or anything else for that matter—she decided to give him a minute to calm down.

It was only after several minutes had passed and they were headed for the Wheatley Community Center where her car had spent the night that she said, "It was a really nice day. Sam and Carter had a great time."

True enough, but she thought the reminder might help to relax him.

He took a deep breath, breathed it out and seemed to

settle down before he said, "I hope they did. My brother and I always had a good time with my dad doing rambunctious stuff like today."

"I thought you played outdoor chess with your dad? That's not what I'd consider 'rambunctious.'"

"He's a man of many facets, my dad." And talking about him seemed to lighten Sawyer's mood. "We did play outdoor chess," he went on. "We played inside, too. But we also bowled and drove go-carts and went water-skiing and camping and fishing and snow skiing and hiking and spent many a winter weekend at indoor versions of places like Adventure Kingdom. In some ways my dad was as much a kid as we were."

"You and your brother? There weren't any other kids?"

"Just me and my brother," he confirmed.

"Who is also your lawyer."

"And Huffman Consulting's attorney, too. Sean is my legal advisor on *everything.*"

She heard that same ominous note in his voice that she'd heard twice before. Both times in regard to something to do with Sam. And now there it was again. After what had looked like a somewhat heated exchange dropping Sam off.

Something was going on there that wasn't good, Lindie concluded. But still she didn't feel as if she should pry.

So she went back to talking about his childhood and the father he clearly held in high esteem.

"It sounds like you were really close to your dad."

"Still am. Even though he's in Arizona, we touch base almost every day by phone or email or text."

"Never a rough patch between you? Not even when you were a teenager?"

"Oh, sure, there were rough patches when both Sean

and I were teenagers," Sawyer said with a laugh, as if that was obvious. "We were teenagers. Isn't the job of every teenager to give their parents gray hair?"

"So, the fun with your dad stopped then?"

"Not completely. There were still a lot of camping trips and chess games, but you know how it is then, kids want to be with their friends not their parents."

She would have given anything to have had the chance to be with her parents as a teenager but she didn't say that.

"Most of the other stuff we'd done with Dad, we did with friends instead," Sawyer continued.

"Is that when the troublemaker side we have to deal with came out?" she quipped.

He laughed. "I wouldn't say I *made* trouble but I got *into* some. Boys will be boys, you know? But it was actually Sean who was more into causes and politics and petitions. My troublemaking was not quite that organized then."

"What kind of trouble did you get into?"

"It was my dad's fault," he joked, not really laying blame. "That fun we had driving go-carts sort of translated into some drag racing the first summer I had a license. And that camping-out stuff? Let's say that's what sparked sneaking out of my bedroom window to enjoy some long summer nights."

"Alone?"

"Alone until I got to my girlfriend's house," he said with a devilish laugh.

After a day that had been so consumed with the boys and keeping them in tow and supervised and entertained and safe, it was nice to have Sawyer all to herself just to talk and she was dreading reaching the community center and having it end.

She tried to ignore that. "So do you have a police record from drag racing and whatever you did with your girlfriend—kidnapping, corrupting a minor, lewd and lascivious behavior?"

He laughed. "Are you looking for something to smear me with when I'm mounting a campaign against you?"

"Hmm. I hadn't thought of that."

"Sorry, no police record. And it's not 'corrupting a minor' when you're a minor, too. Or 'kidnapping' when the girl willingly sneaks out."

"But it *was* lewd and lascivious?"

She was looking at his profile when she said that so she saw him grin. But all he said was "I got caught drag racing when I drove off the road and into a ravine I couldn't get out of. We were in the middle of nowhere—*not* at the movies where I was supposed to be that night. So while nobody called the cops, I did have to call my dad to come with one of his work trucks to tow me out."

"That would have been the end of driving for any one of us in that situation," Lindie observed.

"For a solid year," he said as if it had been painful. "My parents said if I was dumb enough to drag race I was too dumb to drive at all. They took my license."

"And the girl and the sneaking out?" she asked, unwilling to let him get away without telling her about that.

"That went on for a full three weeks the summer before I turned seventeen."

"Until you got caught?"

"Oh, yeah."

"How did you get caught after getting away with it for three weeks?"

"The longer I did it, the sloppier I got and the later I'd stay out. One night I didn't come back until dawn. My dad was up and there I was, climbing in my bedroom window when he came out to see if his newspaper was there yet."

"Did he board up the window?"

"No, but he was pretty mad. Instead he added a security system that would go off if either Sean or I tried to sneak out. Then, just for good measure, my mom planted really thorny rosebushes outside every window we might ever think of climbing through. I was grounded for the rest of that summer." He paused, sighed at the memory and then added, "It was worth it, though..."

"Really?" She mused at the satisfaction in his tone and his Cheshire-cat smile.

"Oh, yeah," he said again, the smile turning into a grin once more.

"What? Did you lose your virginity when you were sneaking out?"

The grin got even bigger.

"You did!" she said.

But all he would say was, "Totally worth it."

They'd reached the community center and he pulled into the lot.

Her car was waiting where she'd left it the day before and he parked in the spot beside it.

The second stop in motion and the quiet of the car when Sawyer turned off the engine still didn't wake Carter from his sound sleep in the backseat. And even fully aware that she needed to get him home to bed didn't make Lindie in any hurry to end the night.

Sawyer got out and she had to accept the fact that the evening was going to end whether she was ready for it to or not. She got out, too.

Carter was in his own car seat and Sawyer adeptly unfastened it. Then he transferred seat and boy to her car, secured it there and closed the door—all without Carter so much as stirring.

"I'm glad you know what you're doing with that," Lindie said when he was finished. "I would have had to fumble around to figure it out but you did it so smoothly."

"Practice," he said, laying a long arm across the top of her car roof and leaning one hip against the door he'd just closed as if he wasn't in any hurry to say good-night now, either.

Lindie opened the driver's side door but she didn't get in. She stood in the lee of it, facing him.

"Sam said something about you being gone this week," she said.

"Idaho," Sawyer answered with a nod.

Lindie didn't need more explanation than that. It was where the next Camden Superstore was slated to go in. "I heard your people were starting things there. I don't suppose you'd stop even if I asked you nicely," she said coyly.

"People have a right to know the flip side of the coin," he said with a glance around at the heart of Wheatley's decline.

"We were courted by the area," she countered. "They invited us into their suburb as part of *improving* their decaying economy. It's an urban renewal project."

"Uh-huh. But with that *improvement* comes other issues that the side that invited you in isn't talking about. We will be. Because someone *needs* to be."

"It doesn't *need* to be handled the way you handle it—by making us the demon seed being planted in their midst."

That made him smile again. "*Demon seed.* I like that. I might have to use it."

Lindie closed her eyes and shook her head at his incorrigibleness. When she opened them again he was watching her very intently and in a way that was not the look of one enemy at another.

Hoping to use that to her advantage she said, "Come on, let's you and I hash it out without making it into a big deal."

He laughed. "Let's you and I just not talk about it," he countered. "We had a nice day and I'll be gone until next weekend. Let's not waste our time arguing now."

"So you won't be here on Thursday," she said with a nod in the direction of the center.

"Nope," he said with what sounded like real regret.

She wasn't sure if that regret was for missing his usual day there or for not seeing her. Although on second thought it seemed arrogant of her to even think it might be about seeing her. She knew how much the kids at the center meant to him.

"So I guess you're off the hook this Thursday," he said.

"No, I'll still come. My Take Dinner Home program starts this week," she reminded him.

"Ah, that's right. I've been meaning to talk to you about that. Marie said you'd approached her with it. The kids can sign up to cook the meal and package it to take home with them for their whole family, right?"

"Right."

"They get the kitchen and cooking experience here and then also get to provide an already-prepared meal for their family that night. No work for the folks at home for one night and a free meal because you're funding it, if I'm understanding the way you've set it up."

"The *horrible* Camden Incorporated is funding it through one of our foundations that very few people know is us. Marie just thinks it was something I heard about and arranged. So my cover here isn't blown. She still doesn't know I'm a Camden."

"Anybody can sign up and it doesn't matter if the family is large and a lot of portions are needed."

"They just have to give me a headcount the week before."

"That's a pretty slick way of giving out a free meal."

She wasn't sure if he approved.

She also didn't care.

Well, part of her wanted his approval—as much as she wished she didn't. But even if he didn't approve of this in particular she thought it was a small way of helping people in need without hurting anyone's pride, so his approval mattered less to her.

"I got the idea from things you said about the candy bars. Nobody is forced to sign up or to do it. If they don't need or want the meal, they just don't have to. But this way the kids get to cook one night a week for the family, the family has one less meal a week to pay for, and I don't see how there's anything bad about it."

"I don't, either," he said.

Apparently she was just being defensive because he went on to say, "I think it's great. A lot of the budgets around here can use a little relief, the kids can feel pleased with themselves and proud of cooking for their family one night a week, and everybody wins. The subterfuge of not knowing where the money for it all is really coming from bothers me a little, but around here we take what we can get so I won't rat you out."

She'd told herself she didn't need or want his approval, but it felt pretty good anyway.

"So you think it's okay?" she heard herself say.

"I do. Better than sending vending-machine candy bars home hidden in backpacks."

"There'll be dessert," she informed him.

He laughed and there was no doubt about it, she loved the sound and those lines at the corners of his eyes.

"Good," he said as if dessert were inconsequential. "How long is the program going to last?"

"Indefinitely. I've set it up through the foundation so the funding will go on until the center wants it stopped. And I have a standing order for the take-out containers to be delivered every two weeks until otherwise notified, too, with the bill going to the foundation."

"You're overseeing the cooking on Thursdays?"

"Growing up, all ten of us kids fixed dinner every night with GiGi. I'm just going to do it the way we did."

"A better childhood skill translation than go-carts to drag racing," he conceded.

"Wait, wait, wait," she said, feigning shock. "Was that a *not*-negative comment about the Camdens?"

His smile was sheepish. "Maybe."

"That's it? That's the best I get? *Maybe?*"

His smile this time was slow and thoughtful as his eyes stayed on hers, holding hers. "Maybe you're not such a bad Camden?" he teased.

"Oh, that's very generous of you," she countered facetiously.

"I'm gonna miss Thursday," he said.

This time she had the distinct sense that he was talking about her.

"Don't go to Idaho, then," she challenged. But this time she wasn't thinking about business, she was thinking about the fact that she wouldn't see him.

"Have to," he answered remorsefully. "But maybe I'll

call Thursday night to see how your program went on its maiden voyage."

She knew he was only using the program as an excuse to call. But she was so glad that she'd at least talk to him this week that that was all she could think about.

"Okay," she said softly.

"Okay," he repeated just as softly, still looking into her eyes.

Was he standing closer than he had been? she wondered.

He must have been because all it took was the bend of his elbow on the top of her car for his hand to reach the back of her neck.

And once it was there, only the slightest pressure brought her head up a little more and him nearer still.

Near enough to lean in just enough to press his mouth to hers.

And then they were kissing. Really, really kissing. With lips parted and breath mingling and a slight sway that went on and on and made it so, so much better than that quick buss of Friday night, and so, so, *sooo* much better than that peck on the forehead the night before.

And yes, the man could kiss! If she'd ever had a better kiss she couldn't recall it. This was a kiss that carried her away on the cool night air and told her he just might hate that they were saying goodbye for an entire week as much as she did.

Then it was over. When her eyes drifted open again it was to look up into those well-formed features mere inches above hers, those crystal-blue eyes studying her as if he were committing her face to memory to take with him.

"I should let you get that boy home," he said, his voice deep and quiet.

Lindie nodded, not wanting to go but also now recalling the day and all she'd thought about and the reality that he had Sam.

Yet when Sawyer came in for a second kiss she tilted up her chin and let it happen again. Let it go on and on for a very long time. Let it end only when he did that, too.

He took his hand away from the back of her neck, put his other hand on the top of her doorframe and stepped back so she could get in behind the wheel of her car.

"Drive safe," he advised.

"You, too," she responded before he closed her door and took a step back as she started her engine.

She glanced through her window at him again.

Oh, but he was handsome.

He waved.

She waved back.

Then she pulled out of the parking spot and drove off.

Taking with her the feel of his mouth on hers, a head full of self-recriminations, and the hope that the week ahead didn't drag as much as she was afraid it would.

At least he'd said he would call on Thursday night.

And that left her with far more consolation than it should have.

Chapter Seven

"I really am sorry, Officer. I didn't realize I was going that fast. It won't happen again," Lindie said to the police officer who had pulled her over for speeding.

As in most things, the Camden name could influence a situation—for better or for worse. Today, when the seasoned cop had seen it on her driver's license it had worked to her advantage and resulted in a warning rather than a ticket. Apparently his son managed a department in one of the Camden Superstores.

She honestly hadn't realized she'd been going so fast. But it didn't come as a surprise. It was Saturday and she was excited to get to Wheatley to help paint over graffiti on the fence that blocked the community center's playground from a major thoroughfare.

Alongside Sawyer.

Whom she hadn't seen since the previous Sunday night.

"You, too. And thank you so much," she said when the older man told her to have a nice day. Then she got back on the road, being more conscientious about her driving.

And giving herself a stern talking-to about the realities of things between her and Sawyer Huffman. The only reason she was seeing him at all was to try to get him to take Camden Incorporated on as a client. That way, his business could boom as compensation for what had been done to his father years ago, and Huffman Consulting would stop campaigning against the opening of every Camden Superstore.

Cut-and-dried.

And no reason she should have spent this past week missing him.

No reason for her to have shopped for new jeans that didn't look new, a new tank top and a new sheer shirt to wear over it today.

No reason that she should have had her phone in her hand nearly every minute all day and evening Thursday in case he called. And then no reason to have been so thrilled when he did. Or to have spent a full hour talking to him.

Well, talking and flirting.

Certainly no reason to have taken off work on Friday afternoon to shop for something new to wear tonight.

Tonight, when he took her to the business dinner he'd suggested during Thursday's phone call.

The business dinner that would allow him to tell her what problems he already saw coming in Idaho if his campaign to keep out a new superstore failed.

The business dinner that Lindie swore to herself she was only looking forward to because it would give her another chance to persuade him that working together could be to everyone's advantage.

The business dinner that she also swore would not end with kissing. Regardless of how many times she'd relived Sunday night's kisses or how much she was itching to have them repeated.

Okay, she was driving too fast again.

She eased up on the pedal and tried to counteract her eagerness to get to the community center by doing what she'd also been doing all week—replaying what had happened on Sunday *before* the kissing. When she'd watched Carter and Sam competing over Sawyer.

He's a dad, she must have told herself a million times this past week.

And that put him on her personal no-fly list.

It did. It really did. Firmly, in bold print, on her no-fly list.

The problem was thinking about Sunday before the kissing somehow always led her back to the kisses.

Those powerhouse kisses.

It would have been so helpful if she'd hated the way he kissed.

But, no. He kissed better than any man she'd *ever* kissed.

So much better it was a little overwhelming. She'd completely forgotten herself, forgotten about everything else until he'd ended it both times.

And *he* always had had to be the one to end it because if it had been left to her she might still be kissing him.

She had to contain whatever was happening between them. She had to look at the big picture. The future. The future in which she didn't want kids of her own to compete for their father's love and attention. The future in which—if she ended up with a man who already had kids—that man would be split between those two family groups.

"So stop it or you're going to regret it down the road," she told herself out loud, believing it wholeheartedly.

Yet when she pulled into the community center's parking lot she drove around until she spotted Sawyer's SUV and parked as near to it as she could get.

And when she hurried into the center she wasn't thinking about anything but laying eyes on him again.

Jeans, sweatshirt, tennis shoes—that's what Sawyer was wearing—nothing spectacular.

But still the minute Lindie caught sight of him in the group of people preparing for graffiti cleanup her heart raced and she went like a heat-seeking missile to join him.

Him and Tyler and Eric, who, it seemed, would be part of their team again this weekend.

But whether or not the boys spent time with them didn't matter to her. Because the minute Sawyer saw her and smiled as if she was the only person he was really aware of, Lindie had the oddest sense that all was right with the world again.

A sense that remained with her throughout the day of work.

The fence painting was finished a little after five and again Eric and Tyler lingered around Lindie until Sawyer told them to go home. That amused Lindie.

But mostly she was thinking about dinner so she didn't mind when the boys finally left and she and Sawyer could head for their separate cars with plans for him to pick her up at her house at eight.

She again pushed the speed limit a little to get home as quickly as possible because she wanted to shower and wash her hair. Once she had, she dressed for the evening in the lacy, form-fitting black dress she'd bought the day before. Black hose and four-inch heels completed the outfit that was only subtly sexy while still being acceptable for what she continued to insist to herself was a business dinner.

For her second application of makeup today, she used a slightly darker and more dramatic eye shadow, a touch more blush and a new lipstick that promised it was kissable.

Not that that mattered, because the whole time she was getting ready she was also reminding herself that there would be no kissing!

After blow-drying her hair she pulled it back on one side into a rose-shaped clip and let the other side fall into its natural waves along her face and in front of her shoulder.

She'd barely finished when her doorbell rang and she hurried to answer it, trying to ignore that she was as excited as a teenager embarking on a date with a rock star.

"Oh, *very* nice…" was Sawyer's greeting after giving her an initial once-over when she opened the door.

"Thank you," she said, flattered, before she returned the compliment. Because he *did* look fantastic.

He was wearing a gray suit that couldn't have showed off his broad shoulders to better effect. And the shirt and matching tie that went with it were almost the color of his eyes, making her all the more aware of how gorgeous they were. Plus he was clean-shaved and smelled divine. Altogether Lindie was a little sorry to go out into the world and share him when she sort of just wanted to get him inside and keep him all to herself.

In an effort to thwart that inclination, she didn't invite him in at all and just took her evening bag from the table near the doorway and said, "Shall we go?"

He pivoted on the heels of polished shoes and swept an arm in the direction of her driveway.

Sawyer had chosen the restaurant and given her general advice to dress up without letting her know where they were going. Not until they were nearly there did he tell her he'd made reservations at a place called the Woodbine Inn.

Lindie knew it. It was a fancy restaurant designed to look like a chalet plucked from the Swiss Alps. Set in a secluded cove of evergreens at the base of Denver's foothills, it was very elegant and known for its four-course meals.

"Ah, the Woodbine Inn—out of the way enough to make it unlikely that any of your clients will spot you with a Camden," she chided when he told her.

He grinned but didn't deny it.

Lindie couldn't fault the practicality of his choice, though, when it was also one of the most beautiful and romantic restaurants Denver had to offer.

Not that romance was a part of the equation for dinner tonight, she told herself firmly as they went inside.

Despite the lush, dimly lit ambience of the old-world European-style restaurant, and the glasses of wine that began the meal, Lindie did manage to keep conversation about business.

Idaho was the topic and Sawyer didn't hold back when it came to his criticisms of putting a new Camden Superstore there. He even rattled off staggering statistics on the projection of small businesses failing, revenues and job loss, and property value declines that Lindie tried to counter with the positives that a superstore provided.

They had a healthy debate that lasted through the appetite tray of foie gras, salmon butter, shrimp, olive tapenade, port wine cheddar and spinach mousseline. It lasted through salads. Through two rare filets with fingerling potatoes and sautéed chard. And even through the dessert tray replete with an assortment of fresh fruit, petits fours and pastries.

It wasn't until the drive back to Lindie's house that she steered him toward giving her his thoughts on some kind of compromise—such as how to build and open the superstore with a minimum of damage. That lasted until they were inside her house and taking two glasses of a brandy she'd been given as a gift into her living room.

By then it seemed to her that she'd safely kept their dinner strictly business and could finally relax. And change the subject.

So off went her shoes while Sawyer removed his suit coat and stuffed his tie in the jacket pocket. Then he loosened his collar button, and they settled in the center of her sofa.

"Do you have Sam tomorrow?" she asked, sitting sideways and tucking her feet under her to face him.

Sawyer angled toward her with an elbow braced on top of the back couch cushions and took a sip of the brandy. "I do," he said. "But only for a few hours in the afternoon."

"Are you supposed to have him longer than that?" she asked, interpreting the cause of the edge in his voice.

"I'm supposed to have him more all the way around.

But lately Candy and *Harm* keep coming up with reasons to cut me short."

"Harm?"

"Candy's husband. Harmon. He's a dentist in Wheatley. For now."

For now.

The same words Sawyer had said that first day they'd met. And he'd said them in the same tone, again giving her the sense that something was going on behind the scenes.

This time Lindie decided not to just let it pass the way she had before.

"*Harm* isn't long for Wheatley?" she asked.

"That's the rumor," he said, going on to tell her about more fallout from a Camden Superstore—even medical and dental practices suffered when losses of jobs and livelihoods meant losses of health insurance, leaving them either with fewer patients or with patients who couldn't pay their bills.

"Vermont," she repeated when he told her there was the possibility that his former girlfriend and her husband could be moving.

"That's what Harm and I were…*discussing* when we dropped Sam off last Sunday night."

"Discussing heatedly," Lindie said.

He didn't deny it, merely saying, "Candy, being Candy, won't be the one to tell me anything she knows is going to be aggravating and potentially start a fight. She leaves it to Harm, who, as far as I'm concerned, is *not* who I should be dealing with when it comes to my son. But that's how it is and last Sunday he told me he's putting out feelers to sell his practice here. If there's interest he's going to take the next step."

"Meaning he'll actually sell the practice and move your son to Vermont."

"I'm not losing Sam if I can help it," Sawyer said darkly, going on to talk about his willingness to mount a custody battle for his son. But he also admitted that he could very likely lose. And Lindie could see how much that jarred him.

"I'm so sorry," she said. "Is there anything I can do? We have legions of lawyers and contacts everywhere. I don't know if this Harm person is on Camden Superstores' dental insurance, but if it would drum up some business for him I can see if we can add him. Or… I don't know…*anything*?"

But even as she said it—and meant it—she also knew that she was doing what she always did; what she was supposed to be tempering. She was butting in in an attempt to fix someone else's problems.

Still, though, she felt so bad for Sawyer. And for Sam. And she *was* on a quest to make up for wrongs done in the past. Besides, she knew how important it was to Sawyer to be a good dad, to be there for Sam. And he *was* a good dad. A good dad who could potentially lose his son.

"I have a lawyer," he said in a way that told her to slow down again. "A good custody lawyer who I never talk to without my brother, Sean. Sean is also an attorney and does Huffman Consulting's legal work. But he's helping me wade through the custody issues, too, so I can be sure no base is left uncovered and anything that can be done is being done. But it would still be better if Candy would speak up. I know her and I know she doesn't want to move out of Colorado herself. She never has."

"If she doesn't want to move why wouldn't she say that?"

"I tend to have a pattern when it comes to women," he admitted reluctantly. "They seem like my mom and then they aren't."

"They seem like your mother?"

He laughed. "It isn't the way you make that sound. I don't have some kind of weird mommy complex," he assured her after taking a healthy swig of his brandy. "The thing is, my parents have a great marriage. A genuinely happy relationship."

Lindie was glad to hear that, especially after what had happened with her uncle.

"With all my girlfriends through high school," he went on, "there was a lot of drama and demands and stuff that made me miserable and got our house egged and the air let out of my tires and things that none of my family appreciated. One day when I was a senior my dad was helping me clean wet toilet paper off the trees in the front yard and I was griping about it. My dad suggested that I take a look at my mom and find someone like her instead of the high-maintenance girls I'd been bringing around."

"Advice he gave as much for his own sake, I'm assuming."

Sawyer laughed. "He was pretty disgusted, yes."

"But you took his advice."

"Well, initially I did what any teenage boy would do. I rolled my eyes at him and said thinking about my mom when I liked a girl was gross. But after another couple of crash-and-burns with girls in college, I kind of did start watching what went on with my parents. And what I saw was that my mom is *not* a drama queen. She's an easygoing person. It takes a lot to ruffle her. She doesn't make a big deal out of things that aren't a big deal. But, also, when it comes to my mom and dad's relationship, my mom is pretty accepting of anything my dad wants to do. He wants to plant a garden, she says plant a garden. He wants to take up hiking, they take up hiking. He likes to watch Westerns, she watches Westerns."

"Your dad calls the shots," Lindie summarized.

"Not really, no. When my mom wants something, she lets him know. If she doesn't, she says that, too. She isn't a doormat or a pushover, she's just…agreeable, I guess. Not demanding. Certainly not someone looking to pick a fight or to make trouble. And not hard to please."

"So that's what you switched to looking for?"

"Right."

"But…?" Lindie said what seemed implied.

"But I guess I read women wrong because my string of not-drama-queens hasn't been any more successful. In fact, it's kind of led me to even bigger disasters than house-egging and toilet-papering."

Lindie sipped her brandy. "How long is the string of not-drama-queens?" Not that it was any of her business or something that mattered, but she still had to ask.

"It stretches back to college. That was my first really serious relationship. I met Cynthia at a Christmas party sophomore year and we were together until just before graduation. I wanted to make concrete plans for the future I'd been talking about for a while. The future I thought we both wanted."

"But she didn't."

"And hadn't. We'd never wanted the same things. She just hadn't let me in on her actual plans. She said she'd been playing along because it had made me happy, but when it actually came down to it, she wasn't staying in Colorado, she was going back to Georgia."

"And you really didn't have any idea?"

"In retrospect I could see that she hadn't said any real yes to anything, but I took the lack of a no and her listening and putting in a suggestion here and there, to be a yes. Stupidly, I guess. But if my dad wanted burgers and fries and my mom didn't, she said she didn't—right up front, loud and clear. If she went along with it, it meant she was okay with burgers and fries. My dad didn't need to question it, he could just feel sure she was on board."

"That seems reasonable," Lindie conceded. "But Cynthia—"

"Graduated, went back to Georgia and I started my master's degree feeling disillusioned."

"And brokenhearted?"

He would admit to that only by raising his glass as if in toast before he sipped the brandy again and shook his head. "Then there was Melanie who I married two years after college."

"How long were you married?"

"Three years. Just long enough for me to start talking about having kids and to have her shock me by telling me she wasn't going to do that. That was a lot like Cynthia. I'd said I wanted kids even before we got married and Melanie hadn't said she *didn't* want them so I just assumed she…"

"Did," Lindie finished for him.

"But she didn't. And once that conversation started, out came everything she was unhappy about. All news to me because she hadn't said anything. I'd apparently misinterpreted her not complaining about the house we lived in and my travel for work and a dozen other things as happiness and contentment with our life together."

"When the truth was?"

"She'd been waiting for me to figure out that she didn't

like any of those things. Or much of our life together. But I don't know how I was supposed to catch on to that without a clue from her, because, believe me, I've rehashed it and rehashed it, and she seemed okay with everything. She did agree to marriage counseling where she admitted that she hadn't been open about what she wanted. The therapist pointed out that I shouldn't have been expected to just know. But once she did start saying what she wanted…" He shrugged sadly. "We both realized that we did *not* want the same things and divorce was the best option for us both."

"So she wasn't really agreeable," Lindie said softly. "She was just pretending to be and waiting for you to read her mind."

"That was the gist of it. She said if I *really* cared for her and was in tune with her the way a husband should be, I would have been able to tell she was unhappy." He sighed, his frustration evident.

"Another broken heart?"

"And some plain old anger thrown in," he confided. In a sadder tone he added, "At least we *didn't* have kids who had to suffer through a divorce."

"And then there was Sam's mom."

"Candy. We lived together for a year. Long enough for me to see both sides of the Candy coin. Side one is that she appears to be agreeable, like my mom, but that's because she can't say no. She'll let herself be taken advantage of by her friends, her family, at work. Whether she likes it or not. And if she doesn't like it, she kind of holds a grudge that can come out later. But she *still* won't say no."

"And the other side of the Candy coin?"

"She will go to any lengths to avoid a conflict or a confrontation."

"Is that part of why she can't say no? Not just because she's a people-pleaser, but also to keep from refusing someone something and having them get mad at her?"

"Bingo!" he confirmed.

"So you're worrying that she won't say no to Vermont, even though she doesn't actually want to go, because she won't face down her husband about moving."

"I am."

"But she has a fight on her hands whichever way she goes because if she agrees to Vermont, she has a custody battle with you waiting in the wings," Lindie pointed out.

Sawyer sighed again. "I did that on purpose, thinking that the prospect of a court battle would be scarier to her than just telling her husband she doesn't want to move. If she's going to have a fight either way, why not pick the lesser battle? I come up on the short end of that one, though, because she keeps just stepping into the shadows and having Harm deal with me, which means he's fighting that battle, she isn't."

Again Lindie felt so bad for him. Commiserating, she said, "I know sometimes people hide who they really are or what they really want at first because they want you... or something from you."

"You've had experience with that?"

She shrugged as if it wasn't a big deal.

Since she didn't offer more, he let it go. "All I know," he said, "is that my mom never makes trouble for my dad and yet he can always trust and believe her. But when it's come to the women I've thought were agreeable? I haven't been able to find anyone who can live up to that standard."

Something occurred to Lindie then and she asked, "Is that why you were worried that if I'd have taken the Murphy girls home with me from the hospital that I might have regretted it and resented them? Why you said you were trying to make sure people don't agree to things they don't really want to agree to?"

"Taking home four kids is a big deal. I didn't want you to wake up the next morning and want to hit me over the head for letting you do it when you were under the influence of drugs."

"Oh-ho, girls have you running scared," she cajoled.

He laughed genuinely again. "A little bit," he said in a way that made her not believe him.

Or maybe it was because he wasn't looking at her with any kind of fear in his blue eyes. Appreciation, admiration, sensuality, maybe. But not fear.

"So tell me," he said, setting his brandy snifter on the coffee table and settling his arm across the top of the sofa cushions, his hand close enough to catch a strand of her hair to fiddle with. "What have I missed that you really want or hate and aren't saying? Did you really want to eat vegetarian tonight and only ordered the steak because I did?"

Lindie laughed. "I grew up in a house with ten kids. Speaking up is not my problem. If it was, I'd have been lost in the shuffle."

"That seems true enough."

"So if those three women had said, 'Hey, blockhead, I hate it when you do that' or 'This is what I want,' would you have tried to do better or tried to give them what they wanted?" she asked.

"Sure, I would have. Like I said, my mom is agreeable not a pushover or a doormat."

"So you just need to find a way to tell the difference between somebody who's what you're looking for and somebody who's just faking it," Lindie summed up.

"You want to come to the rescue and fix that, too, don't you? First you'll get me a custody lawyer or send business to Harm, now you're trying to figure out how to help me read women. You really do have a problem," he teased.

"You remember me telling you about my rescuing problem, so you *do* listen," she said as if solving a part of the puzzle.

Another laugh from him. This one sort of intimate. "I do. But I'm not sure there *is* a fix for the problem I have picking women. After having it happen a third time with Candy I've just been pretty much laying low. But now here I am, sitting with someone I definitely shouldn't be canoodling with—"

"*Canoodling?* I'm not exactly sure what that is," she said with a laugh as she set her snifter on the coffee table, too.

That move pulled her hair out of his grasp but his hand was still right next to her when she sat back again. He used it to sweep her hair from the front of her shoulder to the back, brushing her shoulder in the process. His touch sent tiny tingles through her but she tried to ignore them.

"Yeah, I'm not sure what canoodling is, either," he said, his voice lower than it had been before. "But it sounded better than 'fraternizing with the enemy.'"

"I'm *still* the enemy?" she asked.

"That does get more and more confusing," he said, his voice slightly lower.

"Okay, I guess I like 'canoodling' better than 'fraternizing with the enemy.' I'm considering it headway," she concluded, her own voice a little softer all of a sudden. "On the other hand," she mused, "I have spoken up about what I want from you."

"I'm not taking Camden Inc. on as a client," he managed to say in such a dark-velvet tone that it was actually sexy.

"But here's your chance to prove you can come through when a woman tells you what she wants…"

"Ohhh," he groaned. "You get points for persistence." His smile said that was all she was getting when it came to that. Then his gaze dropped to her mouth and in more of that sexy tone he said, "But believe me when I tell you that I can come through."

And to show her, he leaned in to kiss her.

She kissed him back. A sweet kiss that was over only a moment later when she said, "Are you just shutting me up?"

"I'm coming through," he countered.

"Kissing is not what I spoke up for."

"It wasn't?" he joked, feigning shock. "I guess I really am flawed because I could have sworn it was."

"In your dreams?" she suggested.

"Oh, yeah. Definitely there," he said, coming in for a second kiss. Only this one was less sweet and chaste. This one had some heat and enough staying power to last quite a bit longer before it ended.

Somewhere during that kiss his hand had come up to caress her face and he left it there even when the kiss ended. He looked into her eyes for a moment before he said, "There isn't a *no* I'm missing here, is there?"

Lindie knew there should have been. She told herself to give him one.

But she liked kissing him so much that she'd craved

it the entire week that he'd been gone. When all she'd wanted was to see him and have him kiss her again.

Now that he was right there, ready to kiss her again, his hand brushing her face in feathery strokes, she couldn't say no to herself. Instead she tilted her chin up and kissed *him* this time.

And he wasn't saying no, either, because the arm from the back of the couch came around her to pull her closer while his other hand cradled her head.

His lips parted over hers and hers parted in response.

Even though she'd relived Sunday night's kisses a million times in her mind the real thing was even better than she'd recalled. No, she hadn't been imagining it. He was really, really good at it. And, oh, boy, did she adore the way he kissed.

So much that everything else wafted away and kissing was all there was. His mouth on hers. His tongue coming to meet hers, to toy with hers in the most divine and sensual of games.

Hands and arms moved. His went around her, those big hands splayed to her back, bracing her, massaging her, turning her muscles to mush. Hers went around him so she could fill her palms with that broad expanse of back and let her fingers delve in, so her breasts could press against his chest and be tantalized by the sensation of soft against hard.

And the kissing…

Mouths opened wider and played with more abandon. Tongues became familiar and even friendlier, and Lindie lost track of how much time was passing, just wanting more and more of what just got better and better—

Until he put an end to it.

It almost seemed as if he felt just shy of losing control because he let out a stunned sort of laugh before he pulled her close, her cheek against his chest, and said, "Okay, I think we need some air."

Speak for yourself.

That was what went through her mind but she didn't say it because she knew he was right. She couldn't remember how long it had been since she'd made out like that but she did know that since becoming an adult, those kinds of kisses usually led to a bedroom.

And that was not where this could go, she told herself.

Though the kiss had stopped, neither of them seemed ready to let the intimacy end. Instead they stayed the way they were for quite a while, wrapped in each other's arms, her head nestled to him, his cheek to the top of it while he held her tight enough for their bodies to melt into one another.

Eventually she eased herself out of those big, strong arms she had absolutely no desire to leave at all—now or maybe ever—and sat up and away from him.

"No?" she said belatedly, though her tone was feeble, barely managing the weak joke.

He held up his palms. "Heard it. Got it," he said as if she'd said it an hour ago and they hadn't just done what they'd done.

He stood and grabbed his suit coat to hook over one shoulder while he reached his free hand out to her.

"Show me out, *Ms. Camden*," he commanded.

She slipped her hand into his, accepting his help to stand, too. Then she wondered all the way to her door why holding hands with him somehow seemed inappropriately intimate. Possibly because she liked the feel of his hand around hers more than she wished she did.

He didn't let go of it as they stopped at her front door. He hung on to it and turned to face her.

"Thanks for dinner," she said.

"My pleasure," he responded, gazing down into her face steadily, as if he didn't want to take his eyes off of her. Then he said, "Thursday," as if he'd been figuring out when they'd see each other next.

Or at least that's what Lindie had been thinking about.

But then he said, "After tomorrow afternoon with Sam I'm flying back to Idaho."

Why on earth did it bother her so much to think he was leaving town again?

She tried to contain it and not to show how it made her feel. "For the whole week again?"

"Just until Wednesday. I'll be back Thursday morning, at the center Thursday afternoon. Did you get Marie's email invitation to her Thank-the-Volunteers barbecue Thursday night?"

"I did."

"Are you going?"

"Are you?" she asked.

"I am," he said.

"Me, too."

"So, Thursday," he mused.

"Thursday," she repeated as if it didn't feel like it was a year away.

He tugged her nearer with the hand he was still holding and leaned over to kiss her again. A long, lingering kiss that lasted at least another ten minutes before he straightened, squeezing her hand as if he didn't want to let it go.

But then he did that, too, and Lindie opened her door for him.

"Why do I feel like I want to say I'll call you from Idaho?" he asked.

"You could," she said hopefully, seizing that idea like a lifeline. "You could give me a daily accounting of the pitfalls you're finding there so we can keep them from happening. It could be a test case for how we actually might be able to work together."

"Or we could just talk," he said softly.

That was all she really wanted to do.

"Or we could just talk," she confirmed, feeling slightly traitorous.

He gave her just a bare hint of a smile then, kissed her again and said good-night without making any commitment to those phone calls.

And all Lindie could do was answer his good-night with one of her own and watch him go to his car.

Hating the fact that another four days had to pass before she could see him again.

And knowing it didn't have a single thing to do with the real reason she was supposed to be seeing him.

Chapter Eight

Sunday was the weekly family dinner at GiGi's house—
the big Tudor on Gaylord Street where Lindie had grown
up. Despite the fact that she worked with her brothers,
sisters and cousins, and saw most of them at least once
a day, she still loved it when they all came together on
Sunday night at their grandmother's house. That was
what felt like the center of everything to her. The heart
of all that was really important.

The event was getting larger and larger as the family grew but even that was nice to see. She liked that so
many of them were finding their soul mates and starting families.

There was one thing different about this particular
Sunday, though.

It was the first one she'd attended feeling as if she
had something to hide, as if she was sneaking around

behind all their backs. And it didn't help when she went into the kitchen for a glass of water and happened upon GiGi checking on the roast in the oven, her cousin Cade opening a bottle of wine, and her brother Dylan munching on one of the housekeeper, Margaret's, homegrown and pickled green tomatoes. Because the minute they saw her Cade said, "You're the person we were just talking about. We were all hoping you might show up with Sawyer Huffman ready to sign a peace treaty today."

"He's raising a big fury in Idaho that we really need to shut down," Dylan added.

Lindie made a face as she went to the refrigerator to fill her glass. "Sorry," she said.

"How is it going with him?" her grandmother asked.

Lindie nearly laughed. She would have said it was going great if he wasn't who he was, if she wasn't who she was, and if all the circumstances were different than they were and they were just dating. But they weren't dating.

As it was, her assignment wasn't going anywhere, while her inappropriate feelings for him were rushing ahead at full speed.

But after filling her water glass she turned to face her inquisitors. "I can't even say I'm getting anywhere with him." If she didn't count locking lips with him. Over and over again. And the nonstop thinking she was doing about him that so rarely had anything to do with business or the task she'd been assigned.

If anyone in her family knew what she was really doing with Sawyer she didn't think they could possibly consider it anything but disloyal. That was certainly how it felt to her. But even the guilt tended to fade into the background when she was with him. Then it was all about him and her overpowering attraction to him.

Trying to set aside her conscience so she could focus, she said, "I know he's being paid to represent our competitors because our stores hurt their business and that's just…well, *business*. But when it comes to the mom-and-pop shops, when it comes to the things he says to get the community support to keep us out, I'm seeing firsthand that he has some really valid points."

"Aw, Lindie," Dylan grumbled, "you can't go all tender-hearted on us the way you do. Not with this."

"This *is* business," Cade reminded her. "You have to toughen up."

Lindie glanced at her grandmother. GiGi had said the same thing to her and the look on the elderly woman's lined face reiterated it even before she said, "You were supposed to just concentrate on Sawyer Huffman. On making some sort of restitution."

"And get him over to our side," Dylan put in.

"But to do that I have to spend time with him," Lindie attested. "He would only do that if I volunteered alongside him in Wheatley. And I can't ignore the evidence right there in front of my face of the damage we can do."

"File it away to be addressed later," GiGi advised. "But for now—"

"Get this guy off our backs!" Cade said.

"In a way that makes up for what your father did to get your mother, Cade," GiGi contributed with a subtle rebuke.

"I know, I know," Cade muttered.

"I'm not sure I'm going to be able to get him off our backs," Lindie said. "I honestly don't think the money he could make with us as a client matters to him. But something else has come up that could be a more meaningful way of making amends," she added somewhat tentatively.

Then she told them about the possibility of Sawyer losing his son to Vermont.

"I think it would be a much more valuable compensation to him and to his whole family if we could direct enough patients to his ex's husband's dental practice to keep the man from selling it and moving," she concluded.

She knew it wasn't what her cousin or her brother wanted to hear. But despite the fact that Huffman Consulting gave Camden Incorporated so much grief, everyone in the family genuinely was committed to making up for what had been done in the past. She thought it was likely that that kept both of them quiet for a moment.

Reluctantly, Cade said, "The guy isn't one of the dentists on our company plan?"

"I did some research today to figure that out. I only knew his first name but it's unique—Harmon—and he's the only dentist with that first name in Wheatley so it wasn't hard to put two and two together. And, no, he isn't on our company plan. But if we added him and put up a notice in the employee lounges announcing that he's a new addition to the providers list and welcomes new patients, maybe that would build his practice back up and then—"

"He might not sell it, which means that he would stay put and so would Sawyer Huffman's son," GiGi concluded, sounding as if she liked the idea.

Dylan and Cade did some grumbling about it but conceded that it would probably mean more to Sawyer, and also to his father who was really the wronged party, than giving Sawyer the financial rewards of working directly with Camden Incorporated.

"It might not get him to stop stirring up trouble for the opening of every new store," GiGi said, "but it might persuade him to feel a little more kindly toward us. That's a step in the right direction."

There was more grumbling between Cade and Dylan about how they didn't see that improving anything much when it came to the roadblocks Huffman Consulting caused.

"I'm still working on that, too," Lindie assured them. "I don't think there's much hope that he'll actually take us on as a client but I do keep bringing it up."

"But he isn't going for it," Dylan interjected.

"Not so far," Lindie confirmed. "But I'm also seeing through his viewpoint how important it is that we do some things differently when we go into a community. If we can minimize the damage, it gives him less ammunition against us in the long run, doesn't it?"

"If we aren't his client he's still going to mount a campaign to keep us out because that's what his other clients pay him to do," Cade pointed out.

"But it's still important for us to go into these communities conscientiously," Lindie maintained.

"Nobody's going to fight you on that," Dylan said with a resigned sigh. "But sometimes, Lindie, that Girl Scout in you is a pain in the neck."

"I know," Lindie acknowledged.

"So," Cade said, "not only does it look like you aren't going to get Huffman to back off, but now you want us to fix all the collateral damage? We already go in in advance and offer to buy out—"

"We aren't doing enough," Lindie said before he could go on.

Dylan sighed and looked at GiGi. "I'm thinking Lindie was not the right choice for this particular mission."

"Or maybe," GiGi said as she picked up an appetizer

tray and headed for the door to the dining room, "she's the perfect choice."

Dylan only growled in reply before he snatched another green tomato off the tray and followed GiGi out of the kitchen.

That left Lindie alone with her cousin who was frowning at her. She wondered if what she'd just told him was enough to make him think she was being disloyal.

One way or another it was how she continued to feel.

Then he said in a resigned tone of voice, "I'll put the wheels into motion first thing tomorrow morning with the dental insurance to see if we can get this guy on as a provider. Email me his name and address."

"As soon as I get home tonight," Lindie promised, grateful that no one seemed to be holding it against her that she hadn't gotten them the deal they'd wanted.

"But, please, do *something* that gets this guy to cut us a little slack."

"I'm trying," she said because it was true.

What was also true was that she'd just done something that wasn't altogether easy for her.

When Sawyer had told her that Sam might be moving to Vermont, a part of her had thought that that might be a small loophole in her feelings against getting involved with someone who had a child. That a child who was far away, who would only be a guest a time or two a year, might not present the same complication as a child nearby who was a constant pull.

Then she'd realized how selfish that thought was and she'd pushed it away before diving into her research to see if there were wheels she could put into motion to keep Sawyer from losing Sam to Vermont.

But if it worked, it kept Sawyer firmly on her no-fly list. And plugged up that loophole to put her right back where she'd started.

What followed was another long week.

Well, a long four days until Thursday that *felt* like a full week to Lindie. And then there was Thursday itself that almost felt like another week as time seemed to inch by until she could see Sawyer again.

She hadn't heard from him on Sunday but he'd called on Monday night from Idaho. And Tuesday night. And Wednesday night.

Each call had begun under the guise of business. They'd talked about problems he was projecting would happen there if a Camden Superstore went in.

But that portion of each call hadn't lasted long before he'd asked how her day was, before they'd settled into meaningless chitchat that had been more about flirting than anything.

Then Thursday dawned and still it had felt as if there was so much to get through—work, her meal preparation group at the community center, then Marie's barbecue. All of it either nowhere around Sawyer or in near prox-imity with a lot of other people in the mix. Even carpool-ing with him from the center to Marie's. Because there was a minimum of parking space at the house, it had meant sharing him with another volunteer who'd asked to catch a ride.

Then there was the barbecue itself before they were finally back in his SUV. This time, thankfully, they were alone since the other volunteer's husband was picking her up.

And maybe Sawyer had felt the same frustration that

Lindie had because he didn't rush to turn the key in the ignition. Instead, once they were in the quiet of his car with the doors shutting out the rest of the world, he turned toward her, put his arm along the top of her seatback and said, "Hi," as if he was seeing her for the first time in a very long while.

"Hi," Lindie answered the same way.

She was wearing a red-and-white, polka-dot halter jumpsuit that buttoned in front to a high throat-hugging collar. The collar seemed more prim than the cut-in arms that bared an enticing amount of her shoulders might suggest.

It was to one of her bare shoulders that his gaze dropped before it raised to her eyes again. "I probably shouldn't say this, but I didn't think we were ever going to get away from everybody."

"Trudy needed a ride and it was nice of Marie to have the dinner for the volunteers," she said as if she hadn't been thinking the same thing.

More people came out of Marie's house, which seemed to spur him to sit straight in his seat, start the engine and put some distance between them and the "everybody" he wanted away from.

It also seemed like Lindie's cue to say, "I've done something I hope is okay."

He took his eyes off the road to peer at her. "Sounds like you think it isn't."

"I mentioned it on Saturday night when you told me what was going on with Sam's stepdad selling his dental practice, but we didn't actually talk about it. Then I did some research and found out that Harmon wasn't a provider on our company plan so we got the insurance company to invite him to become one," she confessed.

Another glance. This one showed her his eyebrows were arched. But she couldn't tell if it was in pleasant surprise or alarm.

"That was fast, Ms. Fix-it," he said, still giving her no indication of how he was taking this news.

"Sometimes the Camden name makes people jump," she confessed somewhat under her breath.

"And an insurance carrier with an account like Camden Incorporated is likely to do about anything you want them to do to keep your business."

She shrugged at the truth in that.

He went back to watching the road as he headed for the community center where she'd again left her car. She didn't get the sense that he was grateful but she felt inclined to finish what she'd begun. "He signed on with them. And we put up announcements in employee lounges at every superstore within twenty miles of here saying he was accepting new patients, and giving his address and phone number to steer people his way."

Still no response.

"I don't know if it will solve the problem," Lindie went on anyway, "but I thought that if his practice starts to pick up because he gets a lot of new patients from us, he'll forget the idea of moving and you'll still have Sam here."

"Or you just made the practice more appealing to buyers and gave Harm the chance to raise the price so he'll want to sell all the more."

Everything stood still for Lindie for a moment as that struck her. "Oh. I didn't think of that." The same way she hadn't thought that opening her purse to a panhandler would turn into a mugging.

But it had.

Sawyer reverted to silence and Lindie worried that her

good intentions had backfired. She pivoted in her seat to look at him, trying not to appreciate what a great profile he had or how good he looked in the pale yellow sport shirt he was wearing with khaki slacks.

"I was trying to help," she said. "Usually men in my life want that. I know you didn't seem to, but I didn't think it could do any harm. I guess I should have cleared it with you first."

He took a deep breath and sighed as if he was resigning himself to the way things stood now. "I know your intentions were good. I guess your idea is worth a shot," he said, relieving at least some of her stress. "I suppose if anything might keep them here it's a surge in Harm's practice."

"That's all I was thinking. I'm sorry if I made it worse."

More silence took them all the way to the center where he pulled into the lot and went to the parking spot next to the only other car there—hers.

Lindie had been hoping he might suggest they go for coffee or something—anything—that would give her a little more time with him. Now she wondered if she'd really blown it and he was just going to want her to say good-night and get out of his sight.

But while he didn't suggest they go anywhere else, he did turn off the engine.

That was better than nothing.

"Are you mad?" Lindie asked.

He unfastened his seat belt and turned toward her, putting his arm across her seatback again. "No, I'm not mad. I can see that you thought this might help. And to tell you the truth, if we had talked about it ahead of time, I probably would have told you to go for it. I want Sam here. Bottom line. But Harm's family is pressuring him to move to Vermont and I don't know if anything is going to stop him from going."

"But we can keep our fingers crossed?"

"We can keep our fingers crossed." Then he shook his head, frowned at her and said, "You really do have a do-gooder problem, though, don't you? You just can't resist getting into the middle of things and trying to fix them."

"I'm so sorry. I really, really am," she insisted.

"Men in your life have *wanted* you to do this?" he asked as if he found that difficult to believe.

"For a couple of them it was actually the *only* reason they wanted me," she said under her breath. It wasn't easy to admit that. "And with a couple others it just sort of happened in a way that wasn't planned—those two I fixed right out of my life." She'd tried to joke but her delivery was feeble because the memories were painful.

"Two guys only wanted you for your fix-its?" he asked.

She hadn't wanted to talk about her past relationships and she still wasn't eager to. But she also didn't want him reaching conclusions that might paint her in an unflattering light. Especially since she was worrying that he might think she was a meddler or a pushover. So she opted to explain.

"I met Jason at the end of him getting his master's degree when we were both volunteering for Habitat for Humanity. He wanted a foot in the door of Camden Inc.'s executive training program."

"I've heard about that. They're coveted slots."

She acknowledged that with a slight nod of her head. "What I guess he didn't count on was that we do an extensive background check on applicants."

"And his was different than what you knew of him?"

"Completely. It was nothing like his rags-to-college-on-loans-that-had-left-him-deeply-in-debt story. Jason's parents were upper middle class, and he didn't have any student loan debt at all. And then there was the engagement announcement for him and someone I'd never heard of in a Chicago newspaper. Funny thing," she said facetiously, "but he'd gotten engaged to someone else at the same time he was talking to me about hoping to start with Camden Inc. so he and *I* could get married."

"Ouch."

Lindie took a deep, steeling breath and said, "He was just using me."

"I'm sorry."

"Thanks?" she said with a humorless laugh, not really sure how to answer that.

"So that was one of the jerks. What about the second?" Sawyer asked gently.

"Ryan James. A guy who seemed to try really, really hard and just never caught a break."

"Another sob story?"

"Pretty much." Lindie released a sigh full of self-disgust and embarrassment. "After Jason it would have been a red flag if Ryan had wanted a job. But he didn't. He had a landscaping business of his own. A struggling landscaping business, but still…"

Sawyer guessed. "You gave him money."

"He seemed so nice and he never *asked* for it. In fact, he'd always turn down what I offered until I insisted."

"Why did you insist?"

She shook her head in self-disgust, still angry with herself for the way it had played out. "Well, I had money and he didn't."

"So you paid."

"The longer we were together the more often I'd discover in roundabout ways that his business was on the brink of disaster or he couldn't make his rent."

"He never told you outright himself?"

"Never! Instead I'd hear him on the phone bartering for more time to pay a bill. Or we'd go to his place and the power would have been shut off while he was gone. And even then he'd make light of it, say it was nothing. A little glitch."

"So you paid for more than movies or dinner."

"Then his business tanked."

"And you paid for it not to?" Alarm was building in Sawyer's voice.

"There was no way he would let me keep it going. It just went under. He still didn't want me to get him a job. He was determined to get one on his own. It was just that he'd been working outside, with plants and dirt and grass, and he didn't have the right clothes for the interviews—"

"So you bought him new clothes. How long did this last?"

"A little over a year."

"And by then you really liked him."

"More than that. He'd actually started to talk about marriage. About how when he was on his feet again he'd buy me the kind of ring I deserved."

"Do not say that you bought your own ring."

"I thought about it. But before it got to that he said his mom was sick. I'd met her and really liked her. She said she needed surgery that was going to cost way, way more than her insurance would ever pay and she didn't have the money and he certainly didn't—"

"Stop," Sawyer pleaded. "I can't take it if I have to hear that you wrote him some kind of huge check and he's living on a beach somewhere now."

"I almost wrote him a check," she admitted. "But I wanted to make sure his mom had the best care so I talked to GiGi and she got Virginia an appointment with one of her doctors. But it was a spur-of-the-moment thing—they were fitting Virginia in. So when I couldn't get ahold of Ryan, I called Virginia directly. She didn't know what I was talking about, she wasn't sick at all, let alone in need of surgery."

"Goodbye, Ryan!"

Lindie nodded sadly.

"But again, it had to hurt to think the guy wasn't in it because of you," Sawyer said sympathetically, back-tracking from his victorious good-riddance.

"I was completely gun-shy for over a year after that."

"And then you weren't?"

"I met Ray. The nicest, sweetest guy. I had the best time with him and we had so much in common. He just never seemed to want anything…physical."

Sawyer's handsome face scrunched up. "He was gay," he said as if he had no other explanation for that. "You helped him out of the closet?"

"Sort of. I introduced him to a friend who's openly gay and they hit it off."

"Well, that was nice of you," Sawyer said with a small, wry laugh, as if he wasn't sure what other comment to make.

"Then there was Brad. Who had a great job he was happy in and plenty of money and was clearly hetero-sexual."

"Look at you, playing it safe," Sawyer joked.

"Except for one thing. Brad was fresh from his wife divorcing him. Which Livi warned me about—"

"But you saw this wounded bird and that made him all the more appealing," Sawyer ventured another guess.

"Maybe," Lindie admitted reluctantly. "I did see how downhearted he was and I wanted to cheer him up."

"Of course you did."

"I suppose in a lot of ways I played shrink with him because we talked and talked about what had gone wrong in his marriage. He analyzed it all and he seemed really determined to do better the next time around. So I was thinking that it would all go into a better relationship with me."

"Instead?" Sawyer asked as if he saw the answer coming.

"He went back to his ex because he convinced her that he knew how to be a better husband to her."

Sawyer blew out a long gust of air and smoothed her hair away from her face with the backs of his fingers, lightly brushing her cheek along the way and then settling his hand on the back of her neck. It was warm and strong and comforting and supportive and it felt so good to have him touch her.

"Then to top it all off," he said, "you got mugged trying to help a homeless guy. I think we can pretty safely say that when it comes to you, no good deed ever goes unpunished."

"Maybe you can break the cycle by not being mad at me for trying to keep Harm-the-dentist's practice going?" she said hopefully.

"Are you kidding? After all that I'm pulling for it to work even more just so you can have a win," he claimed with humor, squeezing her neck. "But truthfully, Lindie, you told me you were trying not to swoop in to fix everyone's problems and rescue them."

"And you were right about the Murphy girls. They were all here today and we packed up enough dinner for them to take home to their aunt's whole family. They're doing okay there."

"I know. And their grandmother is out of intensive care and it looks like eventually she'll be able to go home and take them back with her," he told her. "So you're not the sole solution to every problem. And when it comes to me, please try a little harder not to do any swooping in for the rescue. I'm a big boy. I can handle my own problems."

He was the first man she'd been attracted to who didn't want or need something from her. Who was actively opposed to her doing anything for him or giving him anything.

There was something about that that appealed to a part of her that was separate from the do-gooder in her. A part of her that had never been appealed to quite that distinctly before. And somehow it made him even more sexy.

"From here on," she swore, "handle your own problems."

"You being one of them?" he asked as if she had delivered an invitation.

"Does that mean you consider me a problem or that you want to *handle* me?" she challenged, very aware of the sensuous heat on the back of her neck and the confines of the SUV that had them only inches apart.

"Both?" he said, his voice gravelly as he closed the scant distance between them to kiss her.

That initial press of his lips to hers told her how much she'd been on hold since Saturday night. It was the real homecoming that she'd been inching toward every minute since then.

She closed her eyes and parted her lips in answer to

his, raising a flattened palm to his chest to make it all the more tangible.

And then she just let herself go and she thought he did, too. Because almost instantly they were making out as intensely as they had Saturday night, falling immediately into the throes of mouths locked together and tongues toying with each other in wet, wild ways.

There were only the lights of the community center's parking lot and the streetlamps beyond it, and there in the dim glow nothing existed for Lindie but Sawyer and the sweet taste of his mouth, the clean scent of his cologne and the potency of the indisputable masculinity of him.

Her other arm snaked around him, her hand splayed to his back and rode the hills of every muscle, following the valleys they dipped into and drinking in the pure expanse of him.

His hand went from her neck to her back and brought her in closer as his other hand went to her bare shoulder.

That brought a new sense of intimacy to things. Maybe because of the way he was cupping her shoulder, caressing it, rubbing it. And the ripple effect of that was that Lindie felt her breasts swell within the cups of her lacy strapless bra as if they were jealous, as if they were straining for that same attention.

Then his fingertips moved their massage under the first inch or so of fabric over her shoulder blade and that caused her nipples to tighten as if even that slight adjustment meant more.

Suddenly the heat turned up another notch in their kissing and wanting to feel his hands on her breasts was the only thing Lindie could think about.

She sent her hand from his chest to join the other one on his back, holding tightly enough for their fronts to make contact, hoping that might help appease some of the longing for more intimate contact gaining ground in her by the minute.

Then Sawyer flipped his hand over so that his fingertips ran along the edges of her cut-in sleeve. It was the backs of those same fingers that stayed against her skin as he used the fabric as his guide, tracing it up and over her shoulder, then down again to stop near the hollow of her arm, at the very upper and outermost curve of her breast.

He was thinking the same things she was, Lindie thought. He had to be as that scant contact lingered. And if he was waiting for her to pull his hand away, that just wasn't going to happen because she wanted more, not less.

He seemed to understand because he slid his hand farther down and forward a little more so the backs of his fingers pressed against the full side of her breast.

The deep breath Lindie took expanded her chest in his direction—an involuntary response to how good that felt and how much more she wanted.

How much more she wanted so badly that she pulled one of her hands away from his back and began to unfasten the buttons on the high collar that wrapped her throat so prudishly.

They were still kissing and yet she felt him smile just before his mouth opened even wider over hers, his tongue thrust fully inside and he took her hand away from those buttons so he could do the job.

So many buttons just to get to breast level…why had she ever chosen this jumpsuit?

But then the buttons were unfastened and in came his hand to cup her breast over the lacy bra and it was the bra she cursed. She'd considered going without because of the cut of the jumpsuit but had decided against it since Tyler and Eric would be in her cooking group.

So then it was the boys she was cursing in her mind when Sawyer expertly maneuvered that very adept hand of his into one cup.

The distraction of bra-thoughts made the touch come as a surprise and heightened the sensation, spurring a tiny moan from her. A moan that he answered by clasping her breast more firmly, filling his hand with it to overflow between fingers that delved into her flesh as his palm became the cradle for the nipple that was growing granite-hard.

Okay, yes, she'd entertained a few midnight fantasies of being touched like that by him. But nowhere in any of them had it been as good as it really was. He knew how to kiss and he knew just how to caress, too.

Stroking when stroking felt best. Teasing when teasing worked to tantalize her even more. Tugging and gently pinching when her nipple cried out for that, and then rubbing and soothing and altogether driving her slightly out of her mind.

And still she wanted more.

Or maybe *because* of that she wanted more.

Whatever the reason, it was her lower regions that came to life then. That wanted a turn. A touch. Him.

Outside in the park? she thought.

It was dark. The sky was clear. The air warm. The grass no doubt cool.

But that was so exposed.

So maybe the backseat instead.

They could climb back there. It was a big SUV. The windows were tinted.

But even as one part of her was titillated by the idea

of being that wayward, it wasn't how she wanted it to be between them.

It shouldn't be any way between you! a small voice reminded her, forcing her to face the fact that this had already gone much further than it should go.

This was Sawyer Huffman and her interactions with him were supposed to be strictly business. She shouldn't even be kissing him let alone nearly squirming beneath the pleasures of his hand on her breast and contemplating having sex with him in the backseat of his SUV!

What was she doing? she mentally shouted at herself.

And yet for several minutes more she just had to go on doing it because she couldn't stand the thought of losing his mouth on hers, his hand on her…

But as much as she didn't want to lose either of those things, as much as she wanted to take this whole thing all the way to the end, she knew she couldn't. Not now, anyway. And certainly not in the Wheatley Community Center parking lot.

So after another extended moment of trying to brand into her memory the feel of his hand on her breast, she backed away just enough to give him the message that this had to stop.

Instead his grip tightened. Initially, at least. And then he took her nipple between his thumb and index finger to twist ever-so-tenderly just once before he let go and took his hand away.

The kissing ended, too, and he merely pulled her up against him as if he were having trouble letting go of her completely.

"Not the place to do this," he surmised.

And not what they should be doing, Lindie thought.

But she couldn't bring herself to say it so she didn't say anything at all.

But she also didn't do anything to pull out of that embrace because being in his arms still felt too fabulous.

It couldn't go on forever, though, and after a while she inched her hands between them to set her bra to rights and refasten enough buttons to be decent again.

Sawyer got the message, too, and sat back, releasing her and getting out of the car.

Lindie didn't need him to open her door but while he came around she used the time to finish her buttoning as a precautionary measure since what she really wanted was his hands inside her clothes again.

When the passenger door opened, she got out.

"There's some important baseball game on Saturday?" she said as she moved to her car, as if they hadn't just been on the brink of making love.

"Not important, no. It's just an end-of-summer fun thing. Boys against girls. Since I'm not getting Sam again this Saturday I signed on to coach the boys. Marie is coaching the girls. Want to come?" he asked.

"Sure," she answered without needing to think twice as she unlocked her door and opened it. But rather than get in she turned to face him, loving the way the moonlight dusted his oh-so-handsome features and having second thoughts about what she'd just stopped.

"Good," he said pointedly, looking intently into her face, smiling, putting his fingers through her hair to sweep it out of the way before he leaned in and kissed her again. A kiss that was as sexy and intimate and knowing as if they *had* used his backseat, after all.

But when thoughts of dragging him home with her flitted through Lindie's mind she ended the kiss.

"I have to drive all the way home still," she said feebly, as if that was a reason to stop.

"Me, too," he said with a groan.

Another kiss, just as intense and irresistible, before he was the one to finally end it this time.

He stepped away from her as though distance was the only thing that could keep him from kissing her yet again. "Saturday. One in the afternoon," he said, referring to the baseball game.

"I'll be here," Lindie assured him.

"Then maybe afterward—"

She ignored the seductive tone in his voice and completed the sentence. "I can cook you dinner and we can have a serious talk about what it would mean to your business to have Camden Incorporated as a client."

Oh, that had sounded desperate.

But that was how she felt.

He just smiled and ignored her rationale for the invitation with a "Dinner at your place" acceptance, as if he hadn't even heard the rest.

"And talk about business," she repeated as she silently vowed to use that dinner to really, really push for him to work with them—what she was *supposed* to be doing.

He merely smiled as she got behind the wheel of her car and started her engine.

After he'd closed her door and she'd left him behind in that parking lot, Lindie swore to herself that she was going to put every effort into doing the job she'd been sent to him to do. She owed it to her family to devote herself firmly to that goal and to not let up until she succeeded.

And if she couldn't convince him?

Then she might have to call it quits on this mission.

Because what was going on between them just couldn't go on much longer.

Or she knew she would lose herself in a man she couldn't have.

Chapter Nine

"Sean thinks something might be going on between you and that Camden girl."

Knowing his father couldn't see him, Sawyer made a face but kept his voice neutral. "It's just business, Dad," he assured him.

"She's still trying to get you to turn your back on your clients and represent Camden interests, huh?"

"There hasn't been any talk about turning my back on my current clients, but, yeah, she's still trying to persuade me to take on Camden Incorporated."

Sawyer had used his hands-free call feature to contact his parents just to check in on Saturday morning as he drove to Wheatley for the baseball game. He'd been so busy—and so distracted by Lindie—that he hadn't talked to them as frequently as he usually did. In fact he hadn't talked to them since before he'd had breakfast with his brother. And after a few minutes saying hello to his mother and catching up with his father on other things, apparently now they were going to talk about this.

"Seems like… What's her name?"

"Lindie."

"Seems like her trying to get you to work for them has been going on for quite a while. How much time does it take to say no?"

"Oh, I've said no. More than once." To everything work-related. Not to everything he *should* have passed up.

"But she's persistent," his father concluded. "They're like dogs with bones, those Camdens. Take it from me."

"Well, yeah," Sawyer agreed provisionally. "But I also sort of pushed her into volunteering at the community center so she could see for herself the kind of mess their superstores leave behind. She ended up throwing herself into that more than I expected, so that's kept her around, too."

"And gotten you to like her."

Had that come from Sean or was his father hearing something in his voice that was giving him away?

Sawyer didn't know but suddenly he didn't want to deny it. In fact, something in him wanted to test the waters.

"She's…not what I expected. She's a really nice person."

"And none of the Camdens I've seen in pictures is hard on the eyes," his father pointed out.

Sawyer laughed slightly. "She's definitely not hard on the eyes."

"So you do like her."

Sawyer took a deep breath and plunged in. "How bad would it be if I said I did?"

There was silence on the other end for so long Sawyer began to wonder if they'd been disconnected.

Then his father said, "A Camden…" and Sawyer could tell that he was tempering his reaction. "I suppose I'd be a little worried about whether you should be trusting one of them."

"I haven't seen anything about her that isn't trustworthy."

"Seeing it coming is the problem with those people."

Sawyer's hand tightened on the steering wheel. "I know that's how it was in your situation. But I really don't think Lindie is devious. She actually has a little too much conscience for her own good."

Again his father didn't say anything and Sawyer sensed the caution the older man was practicing.

"I'd hate for you to get into something you'd live to regret," Samuel said after a moment. "Something that could hurt your business or cost you more than you think it might."

"What if I was willing to take that risk?" Sawyer asked.

"Are you?" his father countered.

"I don't know," he said honestly.

There was another pause.

Then his dad said, "Getting into anything with the Camdens wouldn't make your clients happy."

"My job can't be my whole life. I have a right to more. And I work hard for my clients. They all know that and it won't change regardless."

"So what are we really talking about here? Are you wondering what will happen if you wanted to bring a Camden home to us?"

"What *would* happen?" he asked as if it was an academic question.

But, wow, was there a heavy silence then.

This didn't seem to be going well.

"I guess I'd have to say first of all that I hope you know what you're doing," his father finally said.

Sawyer wished he could swear that he did. But the truth was he didn't. He only knew that for some reason when it came to Lindie he was helpless to stop what was happening despite knowing that he should. And he'd begun to wonder how much of a problem he would be creating if this thing between them went on.

Because what he *did* know was that tonight things were going to change, and if they went on at all, it wasn't going to be about anything but the two of them.

"And second," his father said, "if positions were reversed and it was our family that had caused harm to theirs, I wouldn't want you condemned for anything I ever did. I'd want you to be judged on your own merit, for your own accomplishments, for the man you are— not for the man I am. So I s'pose I can't be a hypocrite and I'd have to try to do the same thing when it comes to a Camden."

It wasn't an open-arms welcome but it was something. It was something Sawyer appreciated.

"Be careful, son," his father added with genuine concern. "The Camdens are crafty and cunning and sly."

"I know the old guard was but—"

"You can't be sure the new guard isn't, too. It's a hell of a gamble, if you ask me. All the way around—with your business and your whole life." His father sighed heavily. "But if you're willing to take it… Well, you know we'll always stand behind you."

"How much would you hate it?" Sawyer said.

"I'd just be worried for you. For me, any anger is all in the past. Over and done with a long time ago. I got rewarded for going through it by meeting your mom and having you and Sean, so don't pay any attention to that. But keep a look out for yourself for sure."

"I will," Sawyer promised, hoping even as he did that his vision wasn't already too clouded. "I gotta go. I'm at the community center," he said as he pulled into the lot and parked.

"Just make sure you think with the big head, not with the—"

"I know," Sawyer said before his father could complete the warning he'd been giving him since puberty.

They said their goodbyes and disconnected.

For a few minutes Sawyer sat in his SUV, thinking about what his father had said, thinking about Lindie, about how complicated this was.

But then he spotted her car a few rows in front of him and just knowing that she was nearby sent a rush through him like nothing he'd ever experienced over anyone else.

And even though he tried his damnedest, he couldn't tame it.

"Okay. You cooked me one of the best steaks I've ever eaten. Salad, potato, bread—great. Chocolate cheesecake? Decadent! A little hundred-year-old port to top it all off... And I've listened to your whole pitch. Now you listen to me."

After the baseball game Lindie had come home, showered and changed into a simple A-line black knit dress with a bright orange and pink flower print. It was sleeveless, with a scooped neck and a hem that reached just below her knees. She'd left her hair loose and wavy, the way she knew he liked it.

She'd reapplied a light dusting of blush and mascara, and added a soft eye shadow, too. Then, because it was still warm and she knew she'd be staying at home, she'd skipped nylons and put on only a pair of ballet flats so she was comfortable cooking for Sawyer.

When he'd arrived she'd poured pre-dinner glasses of wine while her dogs had forced him to pet them all, and they'd briefly talked about the baseball game in which the girls had won by one run.

But once that was out of the way and the dogs had settled in various spots around the house, she had, indeed, given Sawyer a no-holds-barred proposal for Camden Incorporated.

And he *had* listened patiently.

But now they'd moved from the dining room into the living room where he'd taken her hand to pull her to sit with him on her overstuffed white sofa.

He kept hold of her hand between both of his, resting them all on his thigh in a way that was comforting and sensuous at once. Then he said what he had said multiple times since they'd met.

"No. No, I will not take Camden Incorporated on as a client."

Every word was spoken slowly and was overly enunciated as if to make sure she understood a foreign language.

"I need you to accept that," he went on. "I decided today, thinking about coming here tonight, that I had to put a stop to it once and for all. I'm beginning to feel like a tease. As though I'm leading you on somehow, even though I've been pretty clear. So hear what I'm saying.

Lindie, I will *not ever* work on the side of Camden Incorporated."

"Not even if I guarantee that by doing it you'll be working to make things better for communities?"

He shook his head and rather than addressing what she'd asked, commanded firmly, "Tell me that you've heard what I said."

Lindie took a deep breath and sighed.

"And you will report back to your family that it isn't going to happen," he added.

"They'll be disappointed. We all thought that growing your business by having you work with Camdens would make up for what was done to your father's business years ago."

"Maybe you can count what you did with Harm's dental practice," he offered hopefully.

"Still, if getting Sam's stepfather's dental practice more business doesn't work to keep Sam here—"

"It's important to me that this business of persuading me to go to work for you ends here and now. Put it behind us. Please," he said without waffling.

"You're sick of hearing it," she noted.

"I just want it over with. Because then I need you to tell me where that leaves us."

That seemed like the important part and what all the rest of what he'd said had been leading up to.

Because if they weren't together for her to make the past up to him and subsequently convince him to stop being such a thorn in her family's side, that left them without a reason to see each other.

And only with a whole lot of reasons not to…

She couldn't bring herself to say that, to face it. Not when her hand was nestled so snugly in the cocoon of his hands and they were sitting there together and the entire time she'd been talking business what she'd really been thinking about was how much she wanted him.

"I don't know…" she said quietly. "Do you?"

He chuckled a wry, helpless sort of chuckle and shook his head. "No, I don't. But even though I've told myself a million times that it has to, I don't want it to leave us nowhere," he confessed in a voice equally as quiet as hers had been. Almost a whisper, as if it went against something sacred to say it out loud. "Is that possible? Or am I really, really barking up the wrong tree?"

There *were* so many issues standing between them.

How could they possibly go anywhere together from here?

"We aren't really in a normal situation, are we?" she said, sorry that it wasn't different.

He had on jeans and a pale gray summer-weight cashmere V-neck sweater that accentuated every inch of his very fine torso and made her itch to touch him. Plus he was clean-shaved, he smelled fantastic, and combined with those blue eyes, that sculpted face of his, and the memory of where Thursday night had ended, the last thing she could think about was watching him walk out right now and never seeing him again.

"No, we aren't in a normal situation," he agreed with a sigh. "We're not in a good situation at all. But…" Another sigh. "I don't think I can just walk away. Can you?"

It was not fair to ask her that and then kiss her. Especially not when Thursday night had left her with so much longing for him that a simple brush of his lips against hers was enough to reignite her desire.

She wanted this man in the worst way and the minute their lips met, her hunger for him wiped away all thought of everything that stood between them. There was only him—big and brawny and masculine and sexy—and her wanting him.

"Can we just have tonight and worry about the rest later?" she suggested when he ended the kiss and looked expectantly into her eyes, waiting for her to tell him if she was any more able to walk away than he was.

"So one step at a time?" he said for clarity.

"One step at a time," she confirmed.

He agreed to that with another kiss, taking one of his hands away from hers to brace her head for a kiss that was much more intense.

Intense enough for lips to be parted and tongues to reacquaint like old friends eager to meet again.

Lindie raised her free hand to his chest to feel that sweater and the honed wall of his pectorals through it. So soft over so strong. And she liked it so much.

They went on kissing and kissing and kissing, and it spun her back to Thursday night, reawakening with gusto everything he'd aroused in her then. Her breasts, her whole body, yearned for his touch, and her thoughts were again of relocating—though not to a backseat or the grassy ground outside.

He stopped kissing her as if he were coming up for air and dipped his forehead to rest against the top of hers. "So what's the next step?" he asked in a raspy voice full of clear insinuation about what he wanted that next step to be.

This could be the start of a real relationship…or this could be a single, stolen night for them to share before they parted ways. Lindie had no idea where things would go from here. That made tonight—this moment—very precious to her. It made it important that she have it all at least this once before any of the complications intruded again.

"I have until dinner at GiGi's tomorrow at six," she whispered.

"I only have until noon when I pick up Sam."

Two of the many complications trying to intrude.

Lindie shoved them away and allowed herself to think only of him and how much she wanted him.

"So you could spend the night," she said.

He smiled a slow smile. "That's the next step I was hoping for. If you're sure?"

Lindie smiled, raised her hand to his cheek and tipped her face up to kiss him.

"I'm sure," she said.

Both of his hands rose into her hair, cradling her head to the kissing that was unleashed then. To the hunger that he must have been keeping under control until he knew it could be released.

And it was released. Opening floodgates in Lindie, too, as mouths went wide and tongues went wild and she gave herself permission to forget everything but Sawyer and being with him.

Immediately giving in to one of the many things she craved, she found the bottom edge of his cloud-soft sweater and raised it up his back, breaking away from kissing him only long enough to pull it over his head.

Kissing him again, she tossed it behind the sofa and flattened her palms to the broad expanse of his shoulders, memorizing the feel of taut muscles that arrowed to his much narrower waist.

One of his hands came out of her hair, dropping to her arm, her elbow, skipping across to her side where it didn't hesitate to rise up to her breast.

She'd been tempted to go braless tonight because, yes, getting here had been on her mind. But telling herself that their dinner was about business, she'd put one on—a lacy demi-cup that matched the panties she was wearing.

She regretted it now when even that thin film of lace beneath the not-much-thicker knit of her dress formed what seemed like far too bulky a barrier.

If only there were buttons or a zipper in the dress that she could open…

But it was a slip-on and while she was inclined to do the same thing with it that she'd done with his sweater, she wasn't sure she wanted to be naked in her living room. She wasn't sure what could be seen through the draperies with all those lights on.

So she tore her mouth from his a second time, took his hand from her breast and held it as she got up from the sofa, bringing him along with her.

Off went the lamp on one side of the couch, then the other. Followed by the overhead in the entryway as she passed by it, leading Sawyer to her bedroom.

The night sky was clear, the moon nearly full, and there were three large windows to let in just enough light.

Sawyer let her take him to the foot of her bed but when they got there he yanked her around to face him and re-captured her mouth with his while he wrapped one arm around her and brought the other hand to her breast again.

It felt good even with the obstacle of clothing so Lindie just enjoyed it and explored his own carved-and-cut pecs.

He did have such a fine body…

But just as she was considering ridding him of the rest of his clothes so she could see it all, he tugged her dress up by slow inches until it was ready to be disposed of much the way the sweater had been.

She was a little glad she'd gone with the bra then because he looked when he saw it.

He leaned back a little and gazed down without any reservations, muttering an "Oh yeah" of approval before he met her lips again with a new frenzy that was something almost too primal to be called kissing as he ravaged her mouth and she ravaged his.

He unhooked her bra and cast it aside, taking both of her bare breasts in both his hands, doubly giving her a taste of what she'd been striving for.

Kneading, caressing, he molded those pliable mounds of flesh that fit perfectly in his palms. Her nipples turned to diamonds delighting in everything he did to them.

Then those talented hands abandoned her breasts, taking her shoulders instead so he could playfully push her to fall onto her king-size mattress.

Still standing at the foot of it, he shrugged out of his shoes and socks—taking something from his front pocket to toss onto the bed as he did. Then he unfastened his jeans and gave her another thing she'd wanted since they'd met. The unrestricted view of him completely naked.

If she hadn't been wishing for it since they'd met, one look at him told her that she should have been because he was incredible—muscular and well-proportioned and all man, sporting impressive proof that he wanted her as much as she wanted him.

With a quietly guttural growl he pulled off her panties and joined her, lying on his side to kiss the tip of her chin, the hollow of her throat, the highest crest of her shoulder, her arm, and the dip between her breasts, before he finally took one of her breasts into his mouth while his hand found the other.

And, oh, yes, the man was good at that, too!

Drawing her in, flicking her nipple with the tip of his tongue, teasing with tender nibbles and gentle tugs and altogether building such a need within her that she almost lost control before she remembered she could work a little magic on him, too.

Finding that long, hard staff, she closed her hand around him, exploring, learning what he liked, what drove him to moan and writhe and show her with a growing urgency of his own hand and mouth how crazy she was driving him.

Then, while his mouth still tormented her breast, that hand at the other flattened against her rib cage and smoothed its way down her stomach, between her legs, finding yet another spot that was crying for his attention, and slipping into her to take things up another notch.

There was nothing she could do to slow the desire he ignited in her then or the small climax that rippled through her as an appetizer before his mouth deserted her breast so he could search for what he'd taken from his pocket earlier.

Rediscovering her mouth with his and tantalizing her with a tongue that gave preview of things to come, he unwrapped the condom and sheathed himself.

Then he opened her knees with his and found his way between them, replacing his hand with something so much better that slipped inside as if it were a missing piece of her.

Burgeoning, he filled her, easing so deeply into her that she wasn't sure he would ever find his way out, and staying very still there for a few minutes to let her get the feel of him.

But only for a few minutes before he started to move.

Lithe and limber, powerful, forceful, into her and almost out again, he went from slow to fast to faster with her keeping pace, matching him, rising to him and falling back only to rise once more.

Her legs curled around his waist, her arms held him steadily, and she went where he carried her into a white-hot realm of pleasure that burst so exquisitely it arched the small of her back, angling the way for him to come even more deeply into her. Blinding her with a bliss she'd never known before until she could only cling to him and let it have her for the moment that it lasted.

That moment when she realized it was taking him, too, because she felt him tense above her, in her, under her hands.

That moment that fused them together and then ebbed, flowing out of reach little by little, inch by inch, until they were both spent and breathless.

Slowly, only slowly, did they come back to themselves.

When she was there, Lindie reveled in the softness of her mattress beneath her and the weight of Sawyer on top of her. In the heat and sleekness of him, in his pure potency. She was too weary to open her eyes even as she lost that weight for a moment when he retreated to her bathroom.

Then he returned to lie on his back, to pull her to lie beside him, orchestrating it with arms that held her so tightly that every curve of her body meshed with his and even she couldn't tell where one of them began and the other ended.

Once he had her where he wanted her, one hand went to her head on his chest to comb her hair away from her temple in soft strokes.

He breathed a replete sigh and she felt exhaustion overtake him.

"Well, that was a nice start," he said, his voice passion-gravelly in understatement.

"That was only the start?"

"We have all night, remember?"

She smiled, liking that. "I remember."

"So intermission, maybe a really quick trip to that drugstore down the street for more…supplies, and then act two?"

"Well, since we *do* have all night…"

"Don't worry, in the morning I'll replenish you with pancakes—they're my specialty."

Lindie laughed and craned her head so she could peer up at him. "Somehow I thought what we just did might be."

He grinned. "That, too."

His eyes closed then, his arm around her and his hand at her head growing heavy as he drifted into sleep.

For a moment Lindie laid there studying him, every sharply drawn line of his handsome face, his angular jawline, the thick column of his neck, the cove of his collarbone and the very fine mounds of his chest.

And still she didn't have any sure or certain vision of where they could go from here.

She only knew that there beside him, in his arms, at that moment, nothing had ever felt so right.

Chapter Ten

Sawyer spent from noon until seven-thirty Sunday night with his son, and as he drove home after dropping Sam off he was aggravated with himself.

He might have been with Sam physically, but his head had been with Lindie. And as much as he loved Sam and missed Sam and never felt as if he had enough time with Sam, a part of him had spent these past hours since leaving Lindie missing her and wanting to be with her. And wrestling with guilt for feeling that way when he should have been completely involved with Sam.

But now that his day with his son was over, he had a small morsel of good news, and Lindie was all he could think about. Lindie was who he wanted to tell that morsel of good news to. Lindie was sure as hell who he wanted to get back to.

There weren't plans for that, though.

There weren't plans for anything. From the moment she'd taken him to her bedroom it had just been about the two of them and that one block of time they had together. They'd slept a little—maybe three hours total—between lovemaking and more lovemaking and more lovemaking even in the shower this morning rather than having those pancakes he'd promised.

Then one of her brothers had called to say he was coming over.

Everything between them had come to a screeching halt. And instead of making love again, or making any plans to get together later, they'd raced around her house, tripping over dogs that thought it was some kind of game, to be sure every scrap of evidence that he'd spent the night went with him when he'd rushed out the door with his hair still wet.

Before he'd even known what had hit him, he was in his SUV on his way home and everything had been left hanging in the air.

Maybe some people liked sneaking around or thought that keeping a relationship a secret added spice. But as he left Wheatley on Sunday night and headed for the highway he was thinking that that wasn't for him.

He didn't want to sneak around to be with Lindie. He'd already had enough of that just since they'd met. Enough of keeping her true identity from the people at the community center. Enough of worrying about anyone connected with Huffman Consulting knowing he was seeing her. And he certainly wasn't looking forward to hiding from her family.

He didn't want to have to hide anything from anyone. He didn't want to lie. He didn't want to rush out of her house as if they were doing something wrong and should be ashamed of themselves.

He also didn't want the underlying desperation he'd felt all through last night and this morning. That urgency that made him feel as though he had to maximize every minute they had together and burn every word she said, every vision of her, every kiss, every touch, into his memory to have something of her, of being with her, to hold on to until the next time.

If there was a next time.

That was also something he'd been worrying about since he'd left her this morning. They were just supposed to take it step by step without any guarantee that once one step was taken, there would be another.

But what else could they do?

He hadn't known what he'd expected going into last night. He'd known there was nothing Lindie could say to convince him to accept Camden Incorporated as a client. Or to convince him to stop exposing the downside of their stores coming in. But he'd also hated the idea that once that matter was settled they would go their separate ways and never have anything to do with each other again.

So he'd asked where his rejection of her offer left them. As if she might have some solution.

But she hadn't. Saying they should just go one step at a time wasn't a solution to him. And certainly following her into her bedroom hadn't been.

It had just been what they'd both wanted.

But now they'd had that and he still wanted her—physically and in every other way.

God help him, he still wanted her so much that he knew this was no passing thing. No lark. This was serious.

But it shouldn't be.

She wasn't a demanding diva drama queen like the women he'd been drawn to in his first forays into relationships. Honestly, that had been a pleasant surprise, given that she was a Camden. But she also wasn't like his easygoing, undemanding, obliging mother, either. She wasn't someone uncomplicated who would give him the kind of marriage his parents had. She was stubborn and headstrong and determined.

From the very beginning, that first Thursday at the center, when he'd caught her buying candy for the Murphys, she'd done what she'd set out to do regardless of his disapproval.

Then with the Murphys again at the hospital—if he hadn't threatened to send her home in a cab, if she hadn't been weak and drugged, he doubted he would have been able to keep her from taking those girls home with her that night.

There was also Harm and her idea to get him listed as a provider on Camden Superstore's dental insurance. He'd glossed over the suggestion when she'd initially made it but she'd just gone ahead and done it without so much as letting him know she was going to.

No, none of it had been selfish or self-serving—it had all been self*less* and generous of her. But it sure as hell wouldn't make his life easy if she was an intricate part of it and still went around doing whatever she wanted whether he liked it or not.

Which put her somewhere in between the demanding diva drama queens he knew to stay away from, and what he believed would provide him with a relationship that could have a good give-and-take and a happy, harmonious run.

On the other hand, he realized as he sailed along the interstate, Lindie's stubbornness and willfulness was exposed mainly when she was focused on fixing things. Otherwise nothing he'd challenged her to, nothing he'd thrown at her when it came to pitching in at the community center, had shaken her or caused her to dig in her heels. She'd been a good sport. She'd worked as hard as he had, as hard as everyone else had—that was something he *did* want in a life partner.

And, dammit all, she really did care.

Again, because of who she was, he'd figured she wouldn't. But she did.

And she let him know it.

So really, he realized, he didn't have to worry about her not being up front about things—the way it had been with the last three women in his life. And maybe if that left him dealing with more drama or conflict than his father got from his mother, he'd take that—and whatever minor disharmony might come out of it—as a trade-off. Because the more he thought about it, he decided that he would rather contend with the occasional disagreement than worry that Lindie was suppressing her true feelings or going along with things she didn't really want.

At least he'd end up knowing what she was being stubborn or headstrong about so he *could* deal with whatever he needed to.

And, sure, while there was no doubt that Lindie got carried away before thinking things through—as with her willingness to take in the Murphy girls—he had to admit that he liked that she was so tenderhearted. He admired that in her. It was something else he hadn't expected of a Camden.

There were a lot of things he admired about her...

He liked the way she'd devised the plan to send a free meal home to those in need without it seeming like charity. And to even teach the kids the skill of cooking in the process and the importance—and satisfaction—of helping out parents who were overworked.

He liked the way she'd handled Eric and Tyler's obvious crushes on her—using their attempts to impress her to get them to work all the harder, to contribute in ways they might not have otherwise.

Plus, she was beautiful and sweet and kind and funny and smart and accomplished. She was strong and secure. She stood up for herself. And she was sexy as hell.

It was no wonder he was in as deep as he was.

But that still didn't change the other complications. The even bigger issue of who she was, he reminded himself as he drove.

Being involved with a Camden would not please his clients.

He could probably weather some of the displeasure and spin a connection with a Camden as a way for him to get some inside information that he could use for their benefit. But he was still likely to lose one or two of them. And maybe one or two of the people who worked for him, too.

So certainly getting involved with Lindie wasn't a good business move.

But this wasn't about business for him. And he'd meant what he'd told his father—his job couldn't be his whole life. He had a right to more.

And if he weighed the loss of a couple of clients, of any amount of his business, against having—or not having—Lindie? Having her won out.

But there *was* still his dad.

His father was only marginally supportive of the idea of this relationship. He'd let Sawyer know he was wary. And Sawyer was sure that any connection with a Camden would be a reminder to his dad of the lousy thing the Camdens had once done to him.

He wasn't thrilled to be the one to bring that reminder home.

Plus there was her family.

The Camdens weren't getting what they wanted from him—for him to cease and desist his protests against their opening new stores, for him to work for them rather than against them. He was still going to be their adversary. How would it be if he was an enemy in their midst? Or would he not be allowed in their midst at all? Lindie was clearly close to her family. Would she end things with him to avoid their disapproval?

He took a deep breath, then blew it out slowly, feeling a wave of defeat because those things were all true and none of them paved the way for him to be with Lindie or for her to be with him.

So even though he'd worked out that she actually might be the right kind of woman for him, the answer to how he could have her and the future he wanted was that he still couldn't.

But he wanted her.

More now as he got off the highway, as he neared where he could turn to get to his own loft or keep going toward Cherry Creek to get to her house.

To her.

Something in him just couldn't let go of the idea of getting to her. Of being with her. Again and for more than just another night.

So much more than that. That's what he had to have; he knew it with sudden and clear certainty.

He had to have forever.

Oh, yeah, it was definitely serious.

He was head over heels for her.

It was there in him, just waiting to be recognized, and now he did.

He not only wanted her, he wanted what his parents had—with her. The kind of love and caring and closeness. The kind of companionship. The kind of long life together through good times and bad.

"On an island where there would only be the two of us?" he asked himself out loud, facetiously.

But Lindie wasn't the only one with a streak of headstrong stubbornness. He had to admit that he had a pretty strong dose of it, too. And now that he'd found Lindie, he couldn't *not* have her because of things that were outside of them. Not when what they had when they were alone, what they shared, was so damn terrific. Not when it was everything he'd been looking for his whole damn life.

His dad might have reservations, but by the end of their conversation he *had* accepted the idea that Sawyer might be getting involved with a Camden. And Sawyer knew his parents; he knew that they would never treat Lindie rudely or badly if he brought her around.

Plus he had faith that they would warm up to her when they got to know her the way he had, when they learned what kind of person she really was. They would grow to like her, to love her, to accept her. And maybe then to forget about her being a Camden.

But he was going to continue being Camden Incorporated's opponent.

What was he going to do about that? he asked himself as he drove past the turnoff into the heart of Denver and headed farther along Spear Boulevard toward Lindie's house.

There wasn't a fix for his continuing to oppose Camden Inc.

Which stood to reason, he decided, because if there was any solution beyond him taking them on as a client Lindie-the-fixer would have come up with it. And she hadn't.

But maybe if it couldn't be fixed, they could still navigate it. Or just live with it.

If she was willing.

He knew it might be asking a lot of her—to let him into her life when he might not be let into her family.

But it was still something he knew he had to ask. Because he couldn't refuse himself the best thing he'd ever found.

The person who had somehow come to mean every bit as much to him as his son did.

There was no way he could refuse himself Lindie just because all the pieces didn't quite fit.

He just wanted—*needed*—her too much to let anything stand in his way.

As Lindie drove home from her grandmother's weekly dinner she was glad to have Sunday over with. For a day that had started out so well, it had definitely turned sour.

In Sawyer's arms. In the shower with him. Making love. That had all been such a good beginning to the day.

Just thinking about it helped for the fleeting moment that she let herself relive it.

But then she remembered that at the end of that shower, when it had seemed as if they might have a little more time in bed together, Lang had called to say he was on his way over.

Instantly that had meant no more time in bed together. No more lovemaking. Not even a long, lingering goodbye with promises of phone calls or arrangements to see each other later. Instead she'd had to basically shove Sawyer out the door because she hadn't wanted his car to even be on her block when her brother got there.

Just one quick kiss and he was gone. Literally only minutes before Lang arrived.

Lang, who was followed by Dane, so that they could both tell her the latest news from Idaho. Sawyer was gaining so much ground in his campaign against them that the development team that had initially approached them about building a superstore was now having second thoughts. They were considering pulling their support and siding with the naysayers.

If they did that, Camden Inc. could be looking at costly court battles and delays required to fight their way in now that land had been bought, money invested and contracts in place.

Her brothers had insisted she do something to stop Huffman Consulting through Sawyer.

Do I tell them now or later? Lindie had asked herself.

Then she'd decided to let them know that there was nothing she could do. That Sawyer had given her his final decision on Saturday night and would not take them on as a client or stop his efforts against them.

From there word had traveled within the family and by the time she'd walked into GiGi's house for Sunday dinner everyone knew. And everyone wanted to talk to her about it. To make sure she'd pointed out this or told Sawyer that. To suggest other tactics that might be taken.

And while it was clear that Sawyer was who they were upset with, while no one was angry with her, it still weighed heavily on her that the family fixer had failed to fix the family's biggest problem.

It was enough to make her feel terrible on its own. She had always viewed problems from all angles until she could find a solution. Or hammered at them until she could break the problem down into manageable pieces.

But this time? There was no solution and the problem couldn't be managed.

And to top it off, she'd literally been in bed with the man who was responsible for her failure and for their current and future business problems.

That knowledge brought with it an unbearable guilt and an even more overwhelming sense of disloyalty than she'd had before. It also made her worry about what re-action she might face if anyone ever found out just how far things had gone between her and Sawyer personally. Would they think she'd crossed over to his side and ac-tually done something against them all?

It was just awful. And everything put together led her to feel as if she had no choice but to never see Sawyer again—let alone sleep with him again.

The thought of never seeing him again—or sleeping with him again—had bottomed out her mood completely and turned a day that had begun great into a mess.

She was definitely glad it was over.

Although she still felt completely rotten about every-thing.

Maybe some sleep would help. She didn't know *how* it would help, but she did know that she was exhausted and overstressed and she just wanted to climb into her bed, pull the covers over her head and stay there for at least the next twelve hours.

But that wasn't going to happen because when she turned onto her street she saw Sawyer's SUV parked in front of her house. With him sitting behind the wheel waiting for her.

How was it possible to feel so good and so bad at once?

Take away everything else, everyone else, and Sawyer was exactly who she wanted to have waiting for her to get home. He was who a part of her had been secretly longing for since the minute he'd left this morning. He was who her body ached to be up against again.

So seeing him there waiting for her was good.

But recalling where the rest of this day had gone, how disappointed her family was that she hadn't succeeded in getting him to work for them or in no longer opposing them, how embarrassing it was that she was the only one of them so far not to have found a way to make amends, and having to face the fact that she really did think she had to tell Sawyer they couldn't go on seeing each other was bad.

All bad.

All very, very bad.

She pulled into her driveway and turned off the engine, getting out of her car as Sawyer got out of his.

He looked so much cheerier and more energized than she felt. And so great even in just jeans and a heather-gray T-shirt.

She wanted to walk right into his arms, to lay her head to that powerful chest and let him be the wall that blocked out the rest of the world.

But all she did was smile faintly and say, "Hi, stranger,"

as they met at the bottom of the three steps leading to her front door.

He glanced up and down her street. "Is the coast clear?"

"It had better be since you're here," she answered as she unlocked her door and led him inside.

Her dogs greeted them both enthusiastically. When they'd calmed down and allowed Lindie and Sawyer farther into the entryway, Sawyer said, "Rough day or did I just not let you sleep enough last night?"

Apparently he'd heard the weariness in her voice.

"Rough day," she answered.

She slipped her purse off her shoulder and set it on the table beside the door, putting her hands in the pockets of her tan jumpsuit to keep from reaching for him.

"I hope yours was better," she said, motioning for them to go the living room and trying not to think about their last time on that couch.

"Well, I wasn't the best dad I've ever been today," he confessed. "I think I sort of shortchanged Sam because it was you I really wanted to be with."

"Poor Sam."

"I don't think he noticed. To distract him, I went a little overboard and bought him some robot-thing he's been asking for. After that he really didn't *want* me to bother him so he could play with it. It was mostly just that I felt like I wasn't being the best dad…" He shrugged. "But because it was you who was on my mind, it led me to some revelations as I drove back here after dropping him off, and I wanted to talk to you about them."

"Wow, revelations," she repeated, knowing—because it felt so wonderful, so right—that she shouldn't let him take her hand when he did.

"One thing I wanted to tell you that *isn't* a revelation is that because of what you did getting Harm on your dental insurance he's decided to give his practice six more months to pick up rather than look for a buyer now."

"Because he's hoping to get a better price for it later or because if business picks up he won't move Sam to Vermont?"

"That was unclear," Sawyer admitted. "But for now I'll just hope if business picks up they'll stay. Regardless, I'll be glad for another six months with my kid close by."

"It's not a lot but I guess it's something," she said, thinking that it was such a small win it didn't really count.

"It's something I appreciate," he said, squeezing her hand.

"And then the revelation you had was that my ideas might be better than you thought and you decided to take on Camden Inc. as a client, after all?" she said, pretending hope she didn't feel.

"That conversation is over, remember?" he reminded gently. "No, what came as a revelation was that taking things a step at a time is not going to do it for me because I want to have a whole lot more of you than that."

He went on then to tell her what he'd thought about as he'd driven from Wheatley. About what he believed he'd found in her. About what an incredible person he thought she was and how much he cared about her. About how much he wanted her in his life, how much he wanted a future, a family, with her. And about how he didn't want to have to hide any of what they had together from anyone. That he would rather face whatever consequences came than be without her or keep anything a secret.

He told her about how he thought it might take some

time, but that he was sure his family would come to forget who she was and warm up to her.

About how he was willing to weather any fallout from his clients or in his business.

About how anything was worth being with her.

"No, I won't go to work for your family and I won't stop doing the job I do," he concluded. "But vegetarians marry into meat-eating families, and democrats marry into republican families, and sinners marry saints..."

Marry? He was talking about marrying her?

He took a breath as the wheels of her mind spun, then he squeezed her hand again and continued.

"What I'm hoping," he said, drawing her out of her thoughts, "is that we might all be able to separate business from family. That even if Huffman Consulting is still butting heads with Camden Incorporated in the field, outside of that I can just be 'Lindie's Sawyer' to your family. And I promise you that I will do everything I can to be my most charming, winning, ingratiating self to fit in, to make them all like me and forget what I do for a living."

Tears clogged her throat and stung her eyes and she wanted to ask him if he really was proposing.

But it didn't matter if he was.

Yes, she wanted this man. But at what cost?

In the past she'd been willing to go to any lengths for the men she'd cared about and even now her mind was swimming with ideas of how to diplomatically inject Sawyer into her family. Of how to view Huffman Consulting's work as clues to how Camdens could do better. Of how to point out anything and everything he might have in common with each and every separate sibling and cousin and even with their fiancés or spouses so he might be able to fit in. How to bridge the enormous gap that separated her family and this man. How to fix it all.

But every time she'd gone to great lengths to make things work out with a man, she'd ended up hurt herself and having to regroup and start all over again. With Jason using her to get the career he'd wanted. With Ryan taking money from her. With Ray whom she'd finessed into coming out of the closet. And with Brad whom she'd counseled back into the arms of his ex-wife.

And while she'd been hurt to varying degrees each time, with Sawyer everything was on so much grander a scale.

Since getting mugged she'd been trying to temper the part of her that was driven to fix things. Granted she hadn't been too successful when it came to the community center but taking emotional hits from four men and then a physical beating on a Denver street had left her knowing without a doubt that she had to be more cautious in following her instincts to fix things.

And this time following her instincts—following her heart—involved all of her family and the business that generations before them had built, the business that sustained each and every one of them.

This time following her heart could jeopardize her relationship with the grandmother who had raised her, with her brothers and sisters, with cousins who were as close to her as brothers and sisters.

To her, whatever Sawyer was asking of her, whether it was marriage or not, would *create* a problem. A lot of really big problems. Problems that could ultimately alienate her from everyone she held most dear.

Then what?

Would she leave behind her family? The business that

she was a part of, that was her legacy and provided her livelihood?

Would she leave behind everything and everyone she'd ever counted on? Everything she valued? Everything that she'd strived to be a value to?

Could she live with being the cause of such a rift in her family, in Camden Incorporated?

She'd already suffered enough of a sense of disloyalty as she'd gotten closer and closer to Sawyer. How much worse would it be if she was the source of a break in the family?

Then there was the other part of this. She'd always known that she didn't want a man who already had a child or children with someone else.

He'd already said that he'd shortchanged Sam today. If they did get married, if they had kids of their own, wouldn't that be the same song played again and again? Only sometimes it would be their kids shortchanged and sometimes it would be Sam.

That wasn't something Sawyer even knew was important to her, though. It wasn't something she'd told him about. So it wasn't what she said now. Instead she opted for only addressing the issue he knew about.

"What if nothing either of us does makes any difference and you butting heads with us means that my family never sees you as just *my* Sawyer?" *Oh, but how much I wish you could be* my *Sawyer...* "If you're always just the enemy, I could lose my family."

"Or, if they absolutely can't accept me as part of that family, we could just lead our lives separate from them. You work with all your cousins and brothers and sisters so you see them anyway. For family things, holidays...if you needed to be with them, I'd just stay home."

"Oh, I hate that kind of thing," she said. "And not only wouldn't I get to have you with me but then everyone would wonder if I was telling you things I shouldn't. You would wonder if I was telling *them* things you told *me*. I'd be caught in the middle and eventually they might not even want me at work!"

"We're not spies working counterintelligence, Lindie. I mount *public* campaigns, remember? And we talked about this. It could even be of benefit for me to tell you what problems I see coming and for you to head them off. I've been doing some of that about Idaho. In a way we'd be working together. Just not in the way you all want."

Apparently it wasn't helping in Idaho, but still, maybe he had a point. Maybe she could make her family see it.

At least that was what the problem solver in her thought.

But even as she entertained a small—*very* small—glimmer of hope on that front, there was still the issue of Sam. Nothing could be changed about that and even though it was going to come as news to Sawyer she saw that she was going to have to tell him about it now.

"And you have Sam," she said in what was little more than a whisper.

Sawyer's handsome face pulled into a frown. "Sam? You don't like Sam?"

"I do. But…" She hesitated, wishing she felt differently. But she didn't. So she very carefully told him how she did feel, about how adamant she was about not tying her own future to a man who already had a child or children with someone else.

"And you didn't tell me this?" he asked when she finished explaining.

She knew what button she'd just pushed. Too many

women before her had left him in the dark about problems or concerns until they had become major issues that ripped them apart. And while she didn't want to be another woman who misled or disillusioned him, she could tell that's what he was thinking she was.

"It wasn't a part of this before," she said in her own defense. "This was about me trying to make amends for my uncle stealing my aunt from your dad by hurting your dad's construction company. It was about me trying to do that in a way that was to our mutual business advantage. It wasn't supposed to be personal. It wasn't supposed to be about dating and finding someone to have a future with."

"But now my having a kid is not only a part of it, it's a reason for you to tell me no?"

"It is for me," she said. "You just told me that you shortchanged Sam today because you wanted to be somewhere else. Wouldn't that become the story of Sam's life—and the story of our kids' lives—if we had kids? Wouldn't something always have to give? Wouldn't you have to decide whether to go to Sam's Christmas program or one of our kids' Christmas programs? Or sporting events? Or graduations? Or whatever?"

"Maybe. But those things get worked out. They aren't that big a deal—"

"They're a big deal to whoever is the one getting shortchanged. And it's so much more than that. You saw how Carter competed with Sam that day we were all together. Imagine that being every day for Sam or for another kid you love. Another kid you *need* to be there for, another kid who *needs* to feel like they are the most important kid to you but who can never be sure if that's true. I don't want that kid to be *my* kid. I don't want to watch it, to see my kid or kids worrying if you like Sam more, if Sam is better than they are, if—"

"I wouldn't let that happen, Lindie. Any more than I'd let it happen between two kids we had together."

"I'm afraid that it's built-in to having kids who are only half siblings. I'm thinking of Sam, too. Right now he's everything to you. I don't think he could help but feel unseated if you have other kids, kids you're with every day and tuck in every night. And if things don't work out and he ends up in Vermont…"

She shook her head. And forced herself to take her hand from his, to pull it back, out of his reach.

"If things don't work out with that dental practice," she went on, "and Sam ends up in Vermont while you're here with your new kids—that would make it even worse for him. I don't want that for Sam, either," she said quietly but unwaveringly. "I don't want to be responsible for making him feel what that would surely make him feel."

"The kind of insecurity *you* felt," he said with an edge to his voice. "But just because you felt that way doesn't mean other kids will. And we can be on the lookout for it. Head it off."

He stalled when she'd been shaking her head no through everything he was saying.

Then he sighed, sounding frustrated. "So you put it all together and—"

"This just can't work," she finished for him.

"I think it can. You just won't let it," he said. "Of all the damn things you want to fix, why isn't us being together regardless of anything else one of them?"

If only he knew how badly she *did* want to fix this so she could have him.

She just didn't believe it could be. And part of what

she knew she had to be more aware of was when things couldn't be fixed, when to accept that and not throw herself into something that would likely end badly.

"I don't want to be the cause of Sam feeling the way I did growing up. I don't want to bring other kids into a home where they'll immediately have to compete with your other son. I don't want my kids to feel like they have to share their dad with someone who doesn't feel like part of their family. And, yes, when I put it together with the fact that I don't want to be the one who tears up my own family—"

"Then we try not to do any of that," he said, reasoning again.

"And if we do it anyway?" She shook her head once more. "There's too much at stake. Sam and new Sams and my whole family... And if the damage gets done, it doesn't get undone."

"So it isn't only that you want to fix problems, you're so afraid of causing any that you won't even give us a chance?"

She shook her head, unable to say anything around the lump in her throat that she was trying to tame.

"And that's it?" he demanded, sounding as if he couldn't believe it. "We can't even take it a step at a time? We're just done?"

It was what she'd decided even before she'd come home tonight and found him waiting for her. What she'd decided when she wasn't under the influence of that face she never wanted out of her sight. Or that body she wanted back in bed with her right at that moment. Or the feelings that were ripping her apart to have to deny.

It was the decision she thought she had to abide by in spite of everything that tempted her not to.

"I think we just have to be done," she whispered, her eyes burning like fire as hot tears welled up in them.

For a long while as she fought for those tears not to fall, Sawyer merely sat there, scowling at her, looking as if he wanted to shake some sense into her.

Then he stood. But before he moved away from the couch he said, "So my dad lost the girl and now I am, too…"

Lindie didn't know what to say to that so she didn't say anything at all. And after another long moment of watching her as if he thought things might change if he just waited, Sawyer sighed a disgusted sigh and walked out.

And the sound of her front door closing on what she wanted more than anything made the day that had started so well one of the worst days of her life.

Chapter Eleven

"We'll make it work, Lindie. We might even be able to recruit him over time," Lindie's sister Livi had said saucily, "because you know that when he gets to know us he won't be able to not like us."

"But one way or another," her cousin Jani had put in, "you can't let us be what keeps you from him if he's what you want. We wouldn't ever stand in your way."

A week had passed and it was Sunday night again. Lindie had claimed she was sick and played hooky from her grandmother's dinner.

She *was* sick—sick at heart. And after a miserable, awful, horrible week since Sawyer had walked out of her house, she just hadn't had it in her to go the family dinner. She hadn't been able to face sitting around the table where all of her cousins and most of her brothers had people they cared about sitting beside them while she was alone and secretly pining for Sawyer. She had not been able to face even another few hours of trying to act as if nothing was wrong.

So she'd played sick.

But when the dinner had ended her sister and her cousin had showed up at her door, demanding to know what was going on.

Apparently she hadn't fooled anyone most of the week. Jani and Livi had said that for the first two days they'd written off her mood to her failure to close the deal with Huffman Consulting. But when she still hadn't come out of her funk they'd begun to see that there was more to it. They'd decided to bide their time and wait for her to open up, but missing Sunday dinner was too much and they weren't going to let it get any further. Finally, Lindie had broken down and told them the truth.

The end result had been their reassurance that not even getting together with Sawyer Huffman could change the way any of the family felt about her or treated her.

"It isn't like things are with Dylan," Livi had said, "because we know what your guy throws our way and we see it coming."

"And none of it with him is personal," Jani added.

So it couldn't alter her position or any of their relationships, was their conclusion. And if she wanted Sawyer, they—and everyone else—would be cordial to him and welcome him despite the problems he caused them in business.

"And we'll make sure all the boys are nice to him, too," they'd promised in the same making-a-pact fashion they'd employed growing up as the only three girls facing down seven boys.

That had made Lindie cry, too.

"It'll just be business as usual," Jani had said. "And after-hours we'll turn that off. Whichever side took the hit will put on a happy face and we'll have Sunday dinner. He'll just be your guy, and whoever your guy is doesn't change who you are to us. You'll always be ours."

And they would always be hers. Her family. So important to her that she'd been willing to give up Sawyer rather than risk causing any problems with them.

So important to her that nothing any one of them ever did—or anyone they were ever with—could change her feelings for them.

And if she knew that to be true of her feelings for them, she'd reasoned with herself, then why couldn't she relax and believe that the same was true of their feelings for her?

The more she'd thought about that the more she'd come to believe that she could accept Jani and Livi's comfort and support. That she could trust that with or without Sawyer, she would always be in the heart and lives of all the other Camdens.

She hadn't realized how much she still struggled with those old insecurities she'd felt after going to live with GiGi. Those old worries that if she rocked the boat they might wash their hands of her. Fears that she might not measure up in some way to so many cousins and siblings, that she had to "earn" the love and attention of the few adults in their lives.

And now that her cousin and her sister were gone and she was alone with her thoughts about a future with Sawyer again, it occurred to her just how powerful those old worries and insecurities were.

Powerful enough to only add to her belief that Sawyer's relationship with Sam was a deal-breaker.

So even if she accepted that none of her family would ever snub or shun Sawyer, even if she accepted that none of them would ever stand for her separating herself from them or banish Sawyer or her because of Sawyer, even if she trusted that no one would allow a rift of any kind to develop, there was still that issue that couldn't go away.

Sam.

She leaned against the front door she'd just closed after saying goodbye to her sister and her cousin and sank back into despair.

She wanted the man so much but she just couldn't let herself have him...

Because how could she risk that any child she might have—or Sam—would be burdened with worries and insecurities powerful enough to affect them well into their adult lives?

"I can't," she answered her own thought.

And she also couldn't go on crying, she told herself when tears threatened to start again.

Maybe a shower would help.

At the very least it might get some of the puffiness out of her face before she had to see everyone at work tomorrow.

So she showered then plopped onto her bed with a cold washcloth across her eyes, still thinking about Sawyer.

So much about Sawyer.

About how he looked. Every angle of that handsome face, that crooked little dent in his chin, those crystal-blue eyes, that body...

About how much she wanted to be in that same bed with him again, up against that body, to feel those muscular arms around her, to have her face pressed to his chest...

About how sweet and kind and caring and considerate he was.

About how smart, how calm and patient and reasonable and rational and levelheaded.

About how conscientious and responsible he was.

About how funny he was and how much fun she always had with him.

About how right everything felt when she was with him.

And about how much she wanted to be with him. At that moment and for the rest of her life.

About how, if she ever did have kids, he was who she would want to have kids with.

He was such a good dad on top of everything else, she thought. He was good with Sam and he'd been good with Carter. He'd been fair; he'd done his best to give equal time and attention to both little boys. He hadn't showed any favoritism; he'd given his full concentration to each of them when it had been called for.

But still she'd seen for herself the competition between them, and the way it had led to disappointments and frustrations and resentments.

What if she just didn't have kids? she proposed to herself.

She did keep remembering Sawyer telling her last Sunday night that anything was worth being with her. Now she asked herself if being with him was worth anything to her.

Almost anything—that was the answer.

But she wanted kids. She wanted a family. She always had.

And now she wanted those kids, that family, with Sawyer.

It felt selfish.

But she couldn't escape it regardless of how hard she tried.

She wanted that man.

And she wanted to have kids with that man.

So how was she going to fix it? How could she have Sawyer, have kids with Sawyer, and avoid Sam or her own kids ever feeling any of what she'd felt growing up?

No one had known the way she'd felt growing up. It wasn't as if she'd shouted it from the rooftop. She'd been ashamed of thinking that her grandmother might like everyone else better. Of the times when she'd tried to outshine her cousins and her own siblings to keep that from happening. Of worrying about being overlooked in the crowd.

Sawyer had suggested that they could be on the lookout for it happening. That they could head it off.

Was that possible? If they tried to make sure right from the beginning that Sam knew he wasn't being replaced if there were other kids? If they took every measure to merge Sam and any other kids into one cohesive family—the way she and her brothers and sister and cousins had all eventually come to be?

Was it possible to prevent the suffering she'd gone through and the lingering influence of it if—because she knew what to look for and was watching for it—she pulled out all the stops to make sure that neither Sam nor any other kids felt as if they had to compete for their parents' love and attention?

Was it possible to keep Sam or any of her own kids from ever feeling the way she had? The way friends had felt about their own half siblings?

Maybe they could try...

It was the second glimmer of hope she'd had and this time she clung to it.

Wasn't *trying* to head off problems all that any parent could do for their kids?

All that any parent could do was their best to make their kids feel safe and secure and special in their own right.

All any parent could do was their best.

Certainly it was what she *would* do.

And she knew she could trust that Sawyer would, too.

And if—fingers crossed—their kids and Sam never had the foundation of their young lives shaken the way she had, maybe they could better weather sharing Sawyer.

If Sam had his own room in whatever place they lived, if everything was unfailingly equal, if there was never a bigger deal made of any one kid, or any one event for any one child, if they guarded against anyone feeling shortchanged...

Sawyer *had* said he wouldn't let it happen, she recalled.

And he'd also said that it was him who felt as if he had shortchanged Sam last Sunday, but that Sam hadn't seemed to notice because he'd gone overboard a little with a special gift.

If they went to all those lengths, if they were vigilant, could she feel all right about a life with a man who already had a child?

Or was she fooling herself because she wanted Sawyer so much?

She *did* want him. So much. She couldn't deny that.

But maybe this really could be okay, too. As long as she stayed on top of it. As long as Sawyer stayed on top of it.

It might not be perfect, she recognized that.

It wasn't what she'd planned.

But sometimes life just didn't happen the way it was planned.

"*Most* of the time life doesn't happen the way it's planned," she said as she took the wet cloth away from her eyes and sat up.

She might have planned not to get involved with a man who already had kids but if anyone was worth altering her plans for, it was Sawyer. Sawyer was worth accepting whatever complications came with him.

Sawyer was worth the need to be a little extra watchful over the feelings of Sam and any kids they might have.

Sawyer was worth taking extra pains to blend families.

Being with Sawyer, having Sawyer, she realized, wasn't worth *almost* anything.

It was worth anything at all.

She sat for a moment with that thought, imagining a future with him and her family at Sunday dinners, imagining herself as the instant second mother of Sam and making a place for him in her house and her life, imagining herself having her first precious baby without any of it being a first for Sawyer.

And, no, it wasn't exactly what she'd imagined before she'd met him. But with him in every picture, it was exactly what she wanted now.

If he was still interested in letting her make those adjustments. Because now the question was could she fix the problem she'd created with Sawyer?

That wasn't something that needed to be thought about, it was something that needed action. And she couldn't wait even another minute to take that action.

She just didn't want to take it looking the way she was afraid she might look after two days of sobbing.

She got off the bed and went into her walk-in closet, taking a close look at herself in the mirror on one wall of the space that was really a small room in itself.

The cloth over her eyes had helped some of the redness and swelling, and she thought makeup could help even more. So that was the first thing she did—she fixed her face.

When she'd done the best she could with that, she brushed her hair and opted to leave it in the wild-lady disarray that the natural waves fell into if an effort hadn't been made to tame them as they dried. Then she yanked on jeans and a gray tank top, slipped her feet into a pair of sandals and rushed out of her closet.

That was when it occurred to her that she'd never been to Sawyer's place.

He'd told her that he had a loft in one of the high-rises in lower downtown Denver, but that was all she knew.

And maybe it was better if she called first, anyway, rather than just surprise him.

She left her bedroom to find her cell phone but once it was in her hand she hesitated.

What was she going to say?

What if he didn't want to talk to her?

What if he didn't want to see her ever again?

But she couldn't let herself think about those things. She couldn't let more fear stand in her way now.

So she pulled up his number to place the call and tried to ignore her own rapidly beating heart as she waited for an answer.

When the call didn't go to voice mail, when he did answer, she froze for a split second before she said, "Sawyer? It's me. Lindie."

The sound he made was sort of a laugh, sort of a sigh, sort of sad-sounding. "I know."

Because his phone recognized her number and told him. But at least he'd answered knowing it was her.

"Can we talk?" she asked, terrified that he might say no.

"I guess that's better than you calling the cops on me."

"Why would I call the cops on you? I just wanted to talk and realized that I've never been to your place so I called for an address and directions."

"I'm parked outside your house, Lindie. I thought that's what you were calling about."

She hurried to the window in her living room and peered out the plantation shutters.

Sure enough, there he was, his SUV at the curb in front of her house. She could see him sitting behind the wheel.

"What are you doing out there?" she asked.

"I brought Sam home, headed for mine and somehow my car came here instead."

"To do something I should call the cops for?"

"To sit here and wonder how the hell to get through to you and make this work. Because I really want this to work, Lindie."

"Come in," she said, trying not to cry again, this time with relief and joy and hope.

She ended the call, set her phone down and continued looking through the shutters as he got out of his car.

Watching as he walked up from the curb, she just couldn't take her eyes off of him. He had on jeans and a crew-neck white T-shirt with the long sleeves pushed above his elbows—nothing special and yet she was so glad to see him again that to her he'd never looked better.

He reached her front stoop and she hurried to the door to open it.

"Come in," she repeated when he seemed to stall just outside, closing the door when he did step across the threshold.

Then she turned for a closer look at him and saw faint signs that this past week hadn't been any easier for him than it had been for her. A slight paleness to his usually robust coloring, a slight deepening of the lines at the corners of his eyes, a slight hint of all-round fatigue as if he hadn't been sleeping well.

"I hope to God you didn't call me to talk about business," he said as if he might lose control if she had.

Lindie shook her head. "I called to tell you I'm sorry."

"I guess I need to know for what. Because if it's just an 'I'm sorry but I still don't want anything to do with you,' I don't want to hear it."

He was ragged, very near the end of his rope. His tone, his temper—she could hear the fraying restraint in every word that was laced with weariness, a shadow of anger lying just beneath the surface.

But since she couldn't blame him, she accepted it as no more than he had a right to.

"It's more like an 'I'm sorry I've been such a dope and I want a lot to do with you.'"

His eyebrows went up but he didn't say anything, waiting for an explanation as they stood there in her entryway.

But now that she'd admitted that much to him, the rest flooded out without even considering that they were still standing just inside the doorway. She told him all she'd thought about, what she'd realized, the conclusions she'd reached.

"If you still want to try to work it out," she said quietly when she'd finished, "I do, too."

"I'm not happy that you did what every other damn woman has done to me—keeping your fears to yourself instead of sharing them with me before they became a problem," he said.

Lindie's heart beat a little harder. "I know."

"You blindsided me the same way they did and cut me off at the knees with it."

"I know. But I told you, there wasn't a time or a place or a reason for me to tell you before. It isn't something I go into business meetings and announce, and you were only supposed to be business. I can promise you it'll never happen again—I'm not really the suffering-in-silence type."

"There's nothing else you're keeping quiet about?"

Lindie laughed a little. "No."

"And now you're okay with Sam?"

"I was never *not* okay with Sam. I just don't want him or any other kids I might have with you to come up second place."

"I'm not going to let that happen," he said, sounding more like the man she knew him to be: reasonable, rational, no longer angry. "And everything you said about making sure he has a room of his own wherever we live, making sure he's a part of the family we have—that's all stuff I'd be fighting for if you hadn't come up with it yourself. But I can't stand here—here and now—and say that there will never be a scheduling conflict, that I won't ever have to make a choice of whose Christmas program I go to and whose Christmas program I have to wait to see a recording of."

"I know. I just think—now—that maybe it won't be as much of a big deal to kids who aren't looking at it through my perspective."

"And you'll be able to handle it, looking at it through your perspective?"

"I hope so. I'll try."

"And if it bothers you?"

"I'll throw a fit and you'll definitely know it," she assured him with a smile.

He stepped close enough in front of her to clasp her shoulders in those big hands of his, peering down at her. "Good," he said as if he meant it. "I don't ever want you not to tell me what's going on in your head."

"Right now what's going on in my head is a lot of wondering where we go from here," she said, not wanting to ask if he really had been proposing to her last Sunday night but dying to know.

"I think we go on to your bedroom and—after a while—get some sleep that I don't think either of us has had all week. Then we go on to me probably facing the legion of Camdens next Sunday so we can all prove to you that we can be in the same space as nothing but the people who care about you and the people you care about. You *do* care about me, don't you?"

She nodded.

"And somewhere in there, I think we go on to my telling you that I love you, Lindie Camden. That I've never loved anyone as much as I love you, and you go on to tell me—"

"I love you, too," she said quietly.

He took a deep enough breath for it to expand his chest

and then deflate it when he exhaled as if that was what he'd been waiting to hear.

Then he pulled her up against him, wrapped his arms around her and held her tight.

"And somewhere in there we also talk about if you're going to marry me," he said.

"I am."

"And what kind of ring you want, and what kind of wedding you want, and when and where and—"

But the warmth and strength of his muscular body was infusing her with such peace and comfort—and raising desires she'd been fighting all week—to the point that talking suddenly wasn't what she wanted more of.

"I don't want you to go," she said, apropos of nothing but what she was feeling. "Can you just stay tonight and be with me from here on and we'll just do the rest as it comes up?"

"I can," he answered, tightening his arms around her. "You're stuck with me from here on, like it or not."

"I do like it," she whispered.

He reared back then and when she tilted her face away from where it was resting against his pectorals he kissed her. A long, deep kiss that Lindie let herself drift away on until he ended it and looked into her gaze with those beautiful crystal-blue eyes.

"I really do love you," he said, his voice raspy and full of emotion.

"I really do love you," she countered.

"Don't ever let me lose you again—not even for a week."

"Till death do we part?"

"Not even then."

"Okay," she agreed happily as she rose up enough for another kiss.

Another kiss that only confirmed just how much she belonged with this man.

Business friend or foe, he was most certainly her one and only. And she was never going to let him go again.

So when that kiss ended she took his hand and led him to her bedroom.

Where they could have the start of what she knew would be many years together.

The start of a whole lifetime together.

Just the way she knew, in her heart, they were meant to.

* * * * *

MILLS & BOON®

Want to get more from Mills & Boon?

Here's what's available to you if you join the exclusive **Mills & Boon eBook Club** today:

✦ *Convenience – choose your books each month*
✦ *Exclusive – receive your books a month before anywhere else*
✦ *Flexibility – change your subscription at any time*
✦ *Variety – gain access to eBook-only series*
✦ *Value – subscriptions from just £3.99 a month*

So visit **www.millsandboon.co.uk/esubs** today to be a part of this exclusive eBook Club!